THEIR OUTLAW BRIDE

A BRIDGEWATER BRIDES NOVEL

DELTA JAMES

BRIDGEWATER
BRIDES

Cover design: Bridger Media

Cover graphic: Hot Damn Stock; DepositPhotos: johnanderson

BRIDGEWATER
BRIDES

Welcome to Bridgewater, where one cowboy is never enough! *Their Outlaw Bride* is published as part of the Bridgewater Brides World, which includes books by numerous authors inspired by Vanessa Vale's *USA Today* bestselling series. This is a steamy standalone read. Enjoy!

ℰ LIZABETH

"THE DEFENDANT, Elizabeth Morgan, is found guilty of the charges of cattle rustling, aiding and abetting cattle rustlers, and leading the outlaw gang known as Morgan's Marauders. She is hereby sentenced to death by hanging..." Judge Warren Abernathy droned on.

His voice became a mere buzzing in her head as she heard him pronounce the judgment of the court. Elizabeth had expected to go to prison if caught, not die. Her lawyer stood next to her, with his hand around her waist as if he expected her knees to buckle. Elizabeth took a deep breath and steeled herself. She'd become an outlaw to escape the fate of someone forcing her to her knees as a prostitute. She wouldn't go to her knees now.

"... And may God have mercy upon your soul. Do you have anything to say for yourself?"

In a clear, calm, and cool voice she replied, "Fuck you."

There was an audible gasp from the crowd. They, and the judge, hadn't expected that.

Elizabeth smiled, although it was a struggle for, inside, she was quaking in fear. Still, she had a front that was expected, and she would not see it falter.

"Miss Morgan, a little decorum, please," said the green-behind-the ears lawyer who had defended her.

"Why? What are they going to do, hang me twice?" she asked, pushing past the bailiff and onlookers to saunter past the standing-room only crowd as the sheriff caught up with her to escort her back to jail. Again. She'd been behind bars for three days; the trial rushed because the judge was leaving town to travel his summer circuit around the territory.

"You might try showing a little remorse," said the sheriff as he shoved her through the door to her cell. She was the only female—in fact, currently, the only occupant. The place was dank, bare, and smelled of stale urine and sweat.

"Unlike the hypocrites in this town, I try to keep my lying to a minimum."

"No, you're just a thief," he spat.

The older man had no liking for Elizabeth. The feeling was mutual.

"As opposed to the whore you wanted to make me?" she taunted.

He'd given her the option of sucking his cock instead of going to jail. Elizabeth had gagged at the idea of getting on her knees before the fat, tobacco-chewing asshole and told him she'd rather be behind bars. She began thieving out of honor, and she wore it about her like a mantle. She wouldn't succumb to the sheriff, or any other man. She'd rather die. And it seemed she was destined to do so.

Her mind drifted back to the two men she seen in the crowd earlier during the trial. She'd paid them no mind at that point, but when she'd caught a peek of the duo, one fair, the other dark as night, she'd frozen in place. The bailiff had been forced to nudge her forward to her seat. That one quick peek had been all she needed to set her heart aflutter, just one quick peek. Now, they were men. Big, brawny, well-kept. Their eyes had been squarely on her and, in that split second, it felt as if they'd seen past all the false bravado, past every wall she'd raised to shield her true feelings. She felt as if they'd seen the real her.

"I'm going to enjoy watching you hang." The sheriff's words stirred her from her thoughts of the handsome men.

"You'd better pray I go to heaven because, if I don't, I'm coming back to haunt you, the judge, and every old man on that jury. Maybe I'll even whisper in your wife's ear about all the nasty things you wanted to do to me or, rather, have me do to you. Tell me, Sheriff Gutherie, does your wife let you stick your cock in her mouth, or up her asshole?"

He turned a volatile shade of pink.

Elizabeth laughed as the sheriff sputtered and retreated behind the door into his office. She took a deep, cleansing breath. She'd put him in his place, but she was caught in hers. Behind bars and, tomorrow, with a noose around her neck. Now, how the hell was she going to get herself out of this?

———

GAVAN

Gavan MacLean watched as the sheriff led Lizzie, as he'd begun to think of her, away. His first glimpse of Elizabeth Morgan, the day the trial started, had knocked the wind out of him. Fuck, she was a stunningly beautiful woman; taller than average with a voluptuous figure, green eyes, and long, curly, auburn hair. The pants she wore allowed every male to see her form, which made him want to gouge their eyes out. He knew their thoughts, for they were the same as his own. Those men all wanted to fuck her, get her on her knees, make her beg. Gavan wanted all of that, and more, but he wanted his name on her lips as she came.

Fuck. He shifted on the hard bench seat. Just to be in the same room with her was to feel her pull. One second, he was free; the next, he was shackled to her. The vixen who'd not only stolen cattle across the territory, but whom he feared had stolen his heart as well. And she was the owner of his cock. No other woman would do.

Her mouth spoke of a deeply sensual nature. A man's hands could span her waist, her hips flared wide to aide in both getting her with child and having it safely delivered into the world. Looking at her tits, you knew no child would ever go hungry at her breast.

Ach, Lizzie, take heart. Caelan's here, we'll set things right. I'll nay see you swing,

No fucking way would the only woman who'd ensnared him see another night in jail, let alone worse.

When the judge had pronounced the sentence, Gavan had felt as though someone had punched him in the gut. He worried how it might affect her. She might seem to be stalwart and strong, but he knew it had to be an act and was relieved when she told off the judge. Hell, he'd even laughed.

She exhibited, what he was coming to learn was her normal, defiant attitude, toward the entire proceeding. She was a spitfire of the first order, and everything about her made his loins burn. It was when her mask slipped to reveal the lost little girl behind the façade that his heart broke. It had only occurred a few times, and he'd only observed it because he'd watched her closely. She was brave. Too brave. All he wanted was for her to take refuge within the safety of either he, or Caelan's, arms, preferably both. She wouldn't have to pretend with them. They wouldn't let her, neither in bed, nor out.

Lizzie smelled of heather and sunshine. Each time he saw her, or caught her scent, his cock stirred, something it hadn't done since he'd been cashiered out of the Her Majesty's Army along with his best friend, Caelan MacAllister. The two men had been found *en flagrante delicto* or, conduct unbecoming an officer and a gentleman. That had been a disaster, and he'd been wary since. Until now. Now, he was sure.

Lizzie reminded him little of the women of the MacLean Clan in Scotland. Those ladies might be brash and tempestuous but they didn't make a living rustling cattle and horses with an occasional bank robbery on the side. They might give their husbands a good tongue lashing a time or two, but Gavan had found them dull in the extreme. His Lizzie, their Lizzie, he reminded himself, presented herself to the world as wild and free, mean as a snake with a mouth that would make a sailor blush, a woman who needed the protection and love that only he and Caelan could provide. Some might call it fucking insane, but that was the way of it with his cock, and his heart.

Untamed she might be but, when he'd climbed into bed the night before and closed his eyes, he'd easily pictured her across his knee with her bottom being spanked from ivory to red. A more fitting punishment for her actions, and one he was sure would make her quite contrite.

From there, his visions had shifted to her standing in the corner, her bottom pushed out, cunny and dark rosebud on display before both he and Caelan took turns plowing one or the other together, or one-on-one. Fuck, yes. Thoughts of spanking her, fucking her, watching Caelan fuck her, fucking her together and watching her belly swell with their child, made him hard as a rock. He smiled as he thought that the days of having to provide his own relief would soon be over. And hers for, if there was a woman in need of a few orgasms, it was Lizzie Morgan.

The first day of the trial had revealed that most of the

witnesses against Lizzie had no first-hand knowledge, and some kind of ax to grind. Her lawyer had been a pathetic wimp and never challenged any of their statements. Gavan was disgusted.

With every minute that passed, he could almost feel her sucking him every time the pink tip of her tongue flicked out to lick her dry lips. All he could see was that mouth around his shaft as Caelan drove into her. The difference between all the satisfied women in their past and Lizzie was that he wanted to keep her. For a lifetime. He had a feeling he'd never be slaked by her body, or her wild temperament.

Feisty as she was, he was certain their Lizzie was a virgin. Even though his thoughts ran wild, they'd have to take it slow and easy and give her plenty of time to rest between bouts of their lovemaking. If they showed her gentle, then she'd give them gentle in return. He was sure of it.

When he and Caelan had first agreed to share a bride years ago, they had tossed a coin to see who would relieve her of her maidenhead. Caelan had won the toss but offered to let Gavan breach her cunny first if Caelan could be the first to take her arse.

He'd left the trial at the end of the first day and quickly cabled Caelan.

HAVE FOUND the last item on our list.
    Come quickly. Time is of the essence.
    Don't forget the silver.

. . .

CAELAN RODE through the night and joined Gavan in the courtroom during the scheduled afternoon session of the trial the next day. He slid onto the long bench beside his best friend just before the start of what appeared to be a trial.

"I'm here," he leaned in and whispered. "There's still a section of fence to be done. Let's get out of here. Why don't ye show me this girl so I can get back to the ranch? And why are ye suddenly in such a hurry?"

"We didna need to leave for ye to see our bride," Gavan assured him.

Caelan had looked around. "Who? The lady in the stand over there? She's got to be fifty, if she's a day."

Gavan chuckled. "Didna be daft. Lizzie is our bride." He pointed to the woman who he was convinced was theirs.

"Lizzie?" he whispered back.

"Aye."

"Wait, ye didna mean the lass they have on trial?" His eyes widened, and his mouth actually hung open. "Are you insane?"

"Aye, one and the same," he'd said. "She's perfect."

"She's a cattle rustler and a bank robber..."

"With a glorious figure, red hair, green eyes, and a fiery spirit. Ye've got to watch her." Gavan had lowered his voice. "Good God, Caelan. Think of the sons we'll breed on her."

Caelan might have argued further, but Lizzie had turned to swear at a man who was heckling her from the audience.

Watching his friend, it was all Gavan could do to keep from laughing.

Caelan, who had a gift for gab and was often teased that he should have been Irish, appeared dumbstruck. He couldn't speak, it seemed; he couldn't utter a single word, much less put together a coherent sentence.

Fuck, yes! He'd been right. He was as surprised and fascinated by the female outlaw as Caelan seemed to be.

"As I said, she's perfect, is she not?" asked Gavan.

Caelan nodded. "Fuck, yeah. When ye pick 'em..." Shaking his head, he continued, "Steer rustler, bank robber? What other crimes is she charged with? How are we to make her ours with shackles on her wrists?"

"Then, ye agree?" Gavan asked, ensuring Caelan was on the same page as him, a page on which they would start the new chapter of their lives, all three of them.

His gaze never left Lizzie. "She's a wild one but, there, do ye see it? She's scared as fuck."

Caelan made a funny sound in his throat. "Brave."

Gavan knew Caelan saw it, too. "I figure, when they sentence her, we go the judge and offer to buy out her sentence, like they did with indentured servants. Only one of us will marry her."

His eyes lit up. "Prison or marriage? Yer the best prospect, son of the laird, and all that."

Gavan rolled his eyes at the laird term, for they were thousands of miles, and a lifetime, away from where he'd ever be called that. "Yer sure?"

Caelan had nodded. "I'll not see her behind bars."

After that, the two men had sat silently as they focused and watched the trial.

On the last day, when the sentence was pronounced, both Caelan and Gavan found it difficult to breathe.

"Do something," Caelan hissed at Gavan, who nodded before shouldering his way thought the crowd. "Jail time, maybe, but hung? No fucking way."

"Didna worry," Gavan said, although he was just as fucking furious as Caelan. "I'll handle it. Did ye bring the rings with ye?"

The silver Gavan had referred to in his cable had been a set of matching wedding bands, all with an intricate design they'd had made in Mohamir when they'd first decided to share a wife. They had a diamond and two rubies channel set into their bride's ring.

"Aye, just as ye asked," he said, patting the pocket of his vest. "I'll go to the livery and make sure our horses are ready."

Caelan was as eager and focused as Gavan. Lizzie would be theirs. She just didn't know it yet. And neither did the judge.

"Yer Honor! Yer Honor!" Gavan called in his thick Scottish brogue. "Gavan MacLean."

"Not from around here," the judge muttered before turning to face him. "Now, you've seen American justice at its best, swift and decisive."

It was all Gavan could do not to punch him. He balled his fists and focused on his goal, getting Lizzie wedded to them and her neck safe from a noose. Then, they'd get her in their bed. His balls ached from the wanting of her.

He considers this justice? Gavin thought but held his tongue.

A beautiful young woman was scheduled to die in

less than twenty-four hours, unless he could convince the judge to go along with their plan.

He and Caelan belonged to a communal ranching organization known as Bridgewater. They believed a woman was inherently safer if she was married to more than one man. Life in the Montana Territory was uncertain, at best, and calamity could strike at any time. Having two husbands to guide, pamper, shelter, protect, and cherish her, and any children that might be born of the union, was a concept the men and women of Bridgewater had adopted.

But, if he was to get the judge to approve his plan, he would need to present him with a more conventional proposal than his intention of both he and Caelan being her husbands.

"Actually, no. Surely, ye canna mean to hang her? She's a thief, yes, but not a killer. In fact, she and her gang have never even fired a shot."

"The law is crystal clear; if you steal horses, or cattle, in the western territories of these United States, you forfeit your life, by hanging. The law makes no allowance for the gender of the outlaw," said the judge.

There had to be a way to get the judge to reconsider and commute her sentence. Lizzie was meant to be with he and Caelan. He was sure of it. When Gavan had learned that the leader of Morgan's Marauders was a woman, he'd been as stunned as the rest of the town and went to watch the trial. What had unfolded had been disconcerting, and arousing.

"Elizabeth Morgan wasn't convicted of just stealing. She's been rustling in this area for years. Look, son, I know you're new to our country. But, out here, a man's horse, or his cattle, can be the difference between life and death. There are no exceptions. Well, except for one, and I don't think that applies."

The judge wasn't unkind or, even, Gavan suspected, unsympathetic, he was merely a man who saw the law as absolute but, maybe, just maybe, he was opposed to killing a woman. If so, Gavan could capitalize on this and convince the judge to let him take Lizzie away from there. He and Caelan could provide for her and give her the proper structure and support she needed—the kind that only two husbands could provide.

"What's the exception? Are ye sure she doesn't qualify?"

"Some women in her place would plead their belly, asserting they were with child, and thereby postponing their sentence for at least six months. But, once the child is born, it would be taken away and placed either with a family who wanted it, or in an orphanage, and the woman would be hanged, anyway."

"Has she done that?" asked Gavan.

"No. In fact, when her lawyer suggested it, she punched him in the nose and assured him, and anyone else with earshot, that no man had ever laid a hand on her." The judge shook his head. "She was a feisty thing."

Of course, his Lizzie wouldn't plead her belly and would be offended when someone questioned her virtue. She may have been living a life of crime, but she was not a woman without honor.

"With all due respect, Yer Honor, she isn't dead yet," he said with a bit more bite than he intended.

"No, she's not," Judge Abernathy said, checking his pocket watch. "But, come this time tomorrow, she will have left behind her mortal coil. Perhaps, if she repents, the Lord will accept her into His Eternal Kingdom, and she'll know a peace there which eluded her here on Earth."

There it was, the look of sadness on the judge's face. Gavan was about to bet that the judge would welcome a way to avoid hanging a woman. This was just the opening he needed for his proposal.

"What if..." Gavan started, trying to figure out the best way to frame the question. "What if I could guarantee she'd never trouble you again?" Gavan saw the judge's eyes soften and pressed on. "If I took her away from here to Bridgewater with me and made sure she never returned?"

"I don't know what you have in mind, son, but I'd sooner see her dead than dishonored. I owe her father more than that; we were friends back in the day. Why don't you join me in my office? I think you could use a drink, and I know I need one," he said, hanging his head as his shoulders sagged under what seemed to be the weight of the world.

Gavan tapped down his temper. How dare the judge suggest he would not behave honorably where Lizzie was concerned?

Gavan followed the judge into his private chambers and watched as the old man removed his robe and, with it, his regal bearing. By the time he turned back to Gavan, the latter had poured them each a healthy dose of whiskey. There was more to the judge's reaction than might necessarily meet the eye.

"Ye didna want her to die, either," said Gavan, knowing it was a fact.

The judge nodded. "I knew the family. Terrible tragedy. Indian raid killed all but Elizabeth. Her parents were on the same wagon train as my bride, Beth. Fact is, Elizabeth is named for my Beth. By the time anyone knew about the raid, the Indians had taken Elizabeth. She lived with them for almost ten years."

The judge sighed and shook his head as if trying to rid it of an old, painful memory before he continued, "By the time we got her back, she was damn close to feral. No one could handle her. My Beth had passed on, and I wasn't equipped to take her in. She ended up in a state-run orphanage, until she aged out at eighteen. She had nothing, literally. Given her history, her only real choice was to become a prostitute."

The man called Lizzie's father a friend and suggested Lizzie should have become a whore? No wonder she'd become a rustler.

"Teaching? Religious house?" Gavan suggested.

"Nope. Neither wanted her, and Elizabeth wanted no part of being yoked to a way of life she didn't choose for herself."

"And she didn't want to sell herself, so she began to steal from others."

"That pretty much sums it up. I prayed she'd catch a stray bullet so I never had to sentence her to die."

"What if I took her to Bridgewater with me?" Gavan asked, holding his breath. Now was the moment of truth.

"If I were a younger man, I'd punch you right in the nose. I'd sooner see her dead than made into a whore."

Really? You'd have seen her sell herself instead of becoming a thief and, now that she's facing the noose, you get up on your high horse about seeing her swing before becoming a prostitute.

Instead of saying what he was thinking, Gavan held up his hands, "You misunderstand. I'm nay proposing to dishonor the lass. I'm offering to marry her. Ye could perform the ceremony, yerself, so ye'd know it's legal."

"You'd marry her? Why?" the judge asked sharply, his bushy brows going up, looking Gavan in the eye, trying to read his intentions.

"Simple, I need a wife. Elizabeth has proven she can survive without a lot of frills and would be able to help on the ranch, if needed. Ye have to agree, she's a pretty thing."

The judge seemed to be considering Gavan's proposal.

Gavan let it sink in before continuing, "Then, ye wouldn't have to kill her." He'd set the hook; he'd reeled him in and, now, for the sinker of guilt. "Do ye not think, if she'd had a chance at a normal upbringing, she'd have ended up married to a rancher? I'm offering her, and you, and the memory of her father, that happy ending."

The judge inclined his head ever so slightly.

Gavan's heart soared; he was almost home free.

"What if she won't agree? How do I know you'll treat her right?" he asked.

"You know the reputation of the men at Bridgewater. I

served with Ian Monroe. As for her agreeing, I'll see to that."

"And you'd be willing to do that tonight? Marry her and be long gone before morning?"

"Yes, sir," he said, hoping not to sound too eager. "And, as soon as ye have performed the legal ceremony, I will take the new Mrs. MacLean and be gone, never to return."

"Well, son, if you can get Elizabeth to say 'I do' when I ask her the question, I will be in your debt and will sleep better than I have since this whole mess started."

"Then, we have an agreement?" Gavan asked, holding his breath.

"We do. What do you say to performing the ceremony this evening after the town has settled down? The sheriff and his wife can be the witnesses."

CAELAN

CAELAN LEFT his partner to try and make sense out of the American judiciary. If Caelan was the talker, it was Gavan who knew what to say to bend people to his will. Gavan would see Lizzie free, Caelan was sure of it. His first stop was the livery stable, where he paid the owner for the care of their horses. He considered purchasing a horse for Lizzie, but decided against it. She'd ride in one of their laps. She might as well get used to having a hard cock nestled in the crack of her arse. The very thought of his cock in her arse had the ability to make him hard as a rock. Caelan then went to the general store and picked up supplies, including extra bedding, extra rifles, and ammunition. If Gavan wasn't successful, they'd have to get Lizzie out of town a different way. It wasn't ideal, but they'd break that woman out of jail to make her their bride if they had to.

He smiled. Fuck. A convict for a bride. Who would have ever thought? Gavan had been right. The fiery redhead was not only lovely to look at and amusing to listen to, but she had practically scalped the hide right off the sheriff and the judge. She wouldn't be a boring wife. No, she'd be wild, definitely, but they'd see her gentled. Sated. Happy. It might take a time or two over one or both of their knees, and maybe a cuddle or three, but Caelan had a feeling, when she'd been shown love and kindness, she'd come round and settle down quickly. Faster than a wild mustang, for sure.

Physically, she was far closer to Caelan's preference. He'd always been a sucker for a beautiful redhead. They blushed so prettily, and their skin grew flush when aroused, or when chastised. But, temperamentally, she was all Gavan's. His friend liked them with a fiery, defiant streak that he could mold with the liberal use of corporal punishment, which Lizzie would need. Liberally.

Caelan's cock pressed against the placard of his pants, straining to be free at the thought of watching Gavan with Lizzie. He smiled. On his way to meet Gavan, he'd damned the man for talking him into a moratorium on fucking until they found and wedded their bride. But, now that having Lizzie in their bed, well, in this case, their bedroll, was imminent, Caelan was glad of it. His staff was throbbing in anticipation. She was going to be worth the wait. They'd ensure it was good for her. They were gentlemen, after all but, now that there would be nothing between the three of them, she'd show every bit of her passion. She might be a thief, but she wouldn't steal that from any of them. Her theft of their hearts would be her last act of larceny.

He could easily imagine Lizzie naked. The trousers she'd worn had done little to hide her long, shapely legs, luxurious buttocks, or tiny waist, and her shirt had looked to be bursting at the seams from her large bust. He wondered if her areola would have the kind of peaches and cream complexion most common to redheads, or would they be more of the dark and dusky tones? It didn't matter, he looked forward to sucking her nipples, and her clit.

While he looked forward to fucking his bride's cunny, he wanted to start her arse training as soon as they could. The sooner he and Gavan could fuck her together, the better. They had agreed that Gavan would have her pussy first, but Caelan would be the one to have her mouth and arse first. The idea of holding Lizzie against his naked body, his cock nestled against her arse while Gavan took her maidenhead, was downright intoxicating. Their Lizzie would be well satisfied come morning. If she had one foul thing to say when she arose, that would mean they hadn't done their job as husbands well enough.

 AVAN

GAVAN KNEW he and Caelan would be perfect for Lizzie. She needed someone to guide her, fuck her, and punish her for her naughty ways. The latter would be primarily his job. Caelan's would be to pamper and spoil her, something at which he excelled. There was no doubt in his mind that Lizzie would thrive in their care. Their spirited wildcat would be soothed and tamed by Gavan's steady hand, and the little girl who had lost her childhood would be catered to by Caelan's indulgent nature. As often as her pussy would be stroked, their spitting hellcat would be purring in no time at all.

Gavan entered the sheriff's office, who handed him the key to her cell and headed for the door. "The judge said you wanted time with her. Be careful. She's dangerous."

"Thank you, sheriff. My partner and I will see to all of Lizzie's needs."

Gavan watched the sheriff leave, an odious man if ever there was one.

He entered the cell block, empty, except for Lizzie. She was sitting on her cot, her legs drawn up to her chest, and her arms wrapped around them. She stared off into space as though she had already departed this life. He'd seen men like that after a battle. They went deep inside themselves. Some never returned.

"Lizzie?" he called softly, not wanting to startle her.

No response, not even a slant of her eyes. She needed to learn he was not to be ignored. He was to be obeyed. That started now.

"Lizzie, I'm Gavan MacLean. Judge Abernathy has decided to commute yer sentence."

Still nothing. Well, fuck. That should have gotten a reaction. It seemed his bride to be was going to become Mrs. MacLean and lose her virginity with a bright red backside.

"Lizzie, when I speak to ye, I expect ye to pay attention and answer me," he said sharply.

Slowly, she released her folded-up legs, stretched them out, and turned to face him, sitting with her feet on the floor and her hands gripping the edge of the cot.

His eyes were riveted to her. She was a terrible bit of beauty. And she would soon be his, his and Caelan's.

The eyes she turned to him were haunted and, for a

moment, she looked broken. Then, she straightened her spine, stuck her chest out, and gathered herself.

"First, asshole, my name isn't Lizzie. Second, I don't much care what that old windbag did and, third, I don't give a shit who you are, or what you expect. So, as I'm scheduled to swing in less than twenty-four hours, how about you just fuck off and die?"

"That's enough, lass."

Gavan hadn't anticipated open hostility. After all, he'd just told her she wasn't to die. He stifled the urge to smile and rub his hands together. Yes, taming Lizzie was going to be challenging, inordinately satisfying, and pleasurable. He imagined she'd be spending a fair amount of time over his knee, in the corner, or in their bed. Or, better yet, on her knees sucking one of their cocks while the other one plowed her from behind before they swapped ends. Aye, she needed to understand she would mind them, or pay the price for her disobedience.

"Ye'd better start caring, very much, what I expect from you," Gavan barked at her.

He wasn't a fool. He'd been sure that spanking Lizzie would be integral to her taking her wedding vows. It was a shame she'd lose her virginity with a red and swollen arse, but there was no help for it. She'd been on her own too long, unfettered by convention, or even a steadying influence. He and Caelan were going to have their hands full in more ways than one. Lizzie had a set of tits that would do nicely in that regard; her arse, too, for that matter.

She was built for pleasure. Their Lizzie was tall with an

hourglass figure, long, shapely legs that could wrap around a man when he was giving her a good fucking, and an arse made for fucking, spanking, or both. He'd been having fantasies about the future Mrs. MacLean since the first moment he laid eyes on her. He wanted to kiss those lips, drawing the lower one into his mouth to nibble and suck. He also very much wanted to see them surrounding his cock, or Caelan's, as one of them fucked her mouth. Caelan would be the one to teach her to suck cock. Gavan was looking forward to that; Caelan was an excellent instructor.

The two men had shared more than one woman over the years. With the exception of Bethany, all had flourished under their care. Bethany had been the young bride of their nearly decrepit commanding officer. They were caught red-handed with their pants down, quite literally. Even though she had arranged for them to be caught and had enjoyed the attentions of many others, she'd cried foul. They'd just been the two who were caught.

Bethany had been a selfish little social climber. She had thought she would use Gavan to become the wife of a laird. She had extricated herself from the scandal when she realized Gavan was the second son and wouldn't inherit. It had taken all of Gavan's titled father's considerable influence to keep the Army from charging them both with buggery before summarily dismissing them.

Instead, Bethany had stood by, allowing them to be dishonorably discharged. Gavan's father never spoke to him again. When Gavan had tried to return to the family estate to attend his father's funeral, his older brother, then Laird of the Clan MacLean, had barred him from attending.

"What are you going to do, *asshole*?" she said. "Have me arrested, tried, convicted, and sentenced to die a second time?"

It had been hard to keep his distance during her trial. Time and again, when the lost little girl behind the flinty façade of the outlaw queen had peeked out, it had been hard not to lose another piece of his heart to her, hard not to want to save her, and hard just being constantly hard. His cock wanted what it wanted, and what it wanted was to sink into her wet heat and watch Caelan's do the same. If he closed his eyes, he could practically hear her moaning with desire.

"Nay, lass, yer not going to swing." He let his words hang in the air.

She said nothing but looked at him. Her emotions played across her face, from hope to fear to anger to resignation and back again.

"Why not? Who the hell are you?" she asked, getting off the bed in an aggressive manner.

He chuckled. "I suppose some might call me yer fiancé."

"My what?"

"Ye heard me. The judge has agreed that, in exchange for my marrying ye and taking ye away from here, he will spare yer life."

"I don't give a damn what you and that fat bastard have planned. I'm not marrying you, or anybody else."

Gavan unlocked and entered her cell. Like any other caged and cornered animal, she backed away as he stepped forward, softly saying, "What I have planned, Lizzie, is take yer maidenhead and ride ye long and hard, and then watch my partner do the same. Didna worry, ye'll come hard. We'll always see to yer pleasure too. Ye'll love it, me and Cae will make sure of that."

He had her trapped, pressed into the back wall as he brought his hand up to cup her bottom for the first time. God, she felt even better than she looked. He couldn't wait to have her naked and writhing in his arms. Her nostrils flared, and he watched as the real woman peeked out from behind the mask; shocked, to be sure, but intrigued and aroused, as well.

"In time, I plan to have my cock planted deep in yer cunny while Caelan, that's my partner, takes yer arse."

Her eyes widened, and her breathing became shallow and unsteady as he brushed his hand across her nipples, flicking and then pinching them through the fabric of her shirt. She moaned and swayed against him. No doubt about it, their Lizzie was a woman of fire and passion.

They would give Lizzie a positive outlet for all that fire and passion. Gavan's palm was literally itching to feel her naked bottom underneath it; his cock was becoming unbearably hard at the thought of mounting her and feeling her sheath convulse in orgasmic splendor as he breached her for the first time and shattered her maidenhead.

"Have ye ever watched someone hang?" he whispered. "Unless the hangman is very good at his job, yer neck won't snap, ye'll be left to strangle, twisting slowly in the wind. Ye'll lose control of your bodily functions and will pee and shit yerself. It's not a pleasant way to die."

"What your suggesting is perverse and would pretty much amount to the same thing," she said, recovering her composure.

"Nay, lass. I can see yer intrigued. Ye should be. Caelan and I will see to all yer needs. We'll keep you warm and happy. Ye ken be happy, if ye allow yerself to be. Besides, ye have no choice. I want yer word that ye'll take yer vows when the judge comes to perform the ceremony."

She shook her head. "No and, even if you make me, I'll gut you the first chance I get."

Choosing to ignore her, he said, "Ye'll do nothing of the sort. You either behave, or your first spanking may be with an audience."

———

ELIZABETH

WHO WAS THIS ASSHOLE? Why did she find it difficult to breathe when he was so near? She recognized him as the dark one from the trial, but she'd never had such a visceral reaction to a man. The feeling of his hand gently squeezing her bottom sent jolts of arousal into her nether regions. She'd have rubbed her legs together to ease the ache if he hadn't managed to get one of his thighs between her own.

His thigh was hard and bespoke of power, as did the

hard length that was confined by his trousers. When he moved his hands across her breast, it was all she could do to keep her knees from buckling. She wondered if he had any idea how much she longed to feel him stroke every inch of her body, inside and out.

Gavan MacLean was a tall, heavily muscled man who looked like he'd be more at home in a military uniform than in chaps, boots, and a hat. Black hair, mostly clean shaven, dark eyes, and a voice that could melt molasses. His accent and bearing combined to have her all but melting against him.

Although still a virgin, Elizabeth had more than a passing knowledge of sex. Indians were far more open about the physical aspects of married life, and the men in her gang had often had their sweethearts, or prostitutes, up to their camp. She'd seen more than one man's cock slip between a woman's thighs, seen her arch her back and cry out in ecstasy. Often, Elizabeth had pretended to be asleep, but had rubbed and tugged at her nipples and the little bundle of nerves at the apex of her legs, never quite achieving that ultimate satisfaction.

MacLean had strong hands, she wondered what it might be like to have his hands on her body in place of hers. Would she finally obtain that goal? Would she hear him grunt and groan as he worked his body between her thighs before spending himself in her? Would something as large as the member she felt lodged between them fit deep inside her?

Her bad luck had started as a child and had continued almost non-stop, resulting in her being captured by that toad of a sheriff, the man who had suggested she whore herself for him. She'd sooner have bitten his cock off than sucked it, and the very idea made her want to vomit. But sucking the hard length pressed against her? That might be a different story altogether. She'd seen one of the prostitutes doing that, and the man involved had been groaning in ecstasy. But a cock up her bottom hole? No way.

The sheriff had thrown her into jail. She'd waited for her men to come to her rescue, but they never had. Like everyone else in her life, they had abandoned her. If she was going to be saved, she'd have to do it, herself.

She'd been made to suffer through that farce of a trial. Why had they bothered? Everyone had known what the outcome would be. The whole town pitied her, but not enough to help when it might have made a difference.

"Ye don't really have a choice, lass," he said, gently stroking down her spine and giving her bottom a lingering caress as he backed off. "The judge cares about ye and doesn't want to see ye hanged."

"Really?" she snapped, his physical separation breaking her reverie. "Where was he when my folks were killed? When I was thrown into the orphanage? Or how about when I got tossed out and the only work I was offered was on my back with my legs spread? And, now, I'm supposed to spread them for you to ease his conscience and your lust? Oh, fuck no."

Elizabeth took a deep breath, willing herself not to break down. Rarely in her life had she felt in control, but she would control how she faced the end of her life, and this tall, rugged cowboy who made her legs tremble, pulse quicken, and breathing shallow was not going to take that away from her.

"Lizzie, are ye telling me ye will not take yer vows?"

"You're not too bright, are you, asshole? Yes, that's what I'm telling you. I won't do it, and you and your buddies can't do one damn thing about it. I hope my death is as awful as you describe and you see it every time you close your eyes."

"Count yerself lucky, Lizzie, that I didna have soap and water to wash yer mouth out with. I'm giving ye one last chance to give me yer word ye'll behave and say 'I do' when the judge asks ye."

"Or what?" she said, trying to put as much distance between them as the small cell would allow. "You'll paw me some more?"

"Nay, lass. I didna paw you. I gave you a taste of being pleasured by yer husband, and ye liked it. My guess is the place between yer legs is nice and wet. We'll make sure it stays that way so as to ease the loss of yer virginity."

"Pleasure? You disgust me."

"Lizzie," he reprimanded, "ye'll nae lie to Caelan, nor me. Before I take yer maidenhead, ye'll have come for us and be begging for my cock. And, when I'm through, Caelan will take ye, as well, and you'll be well-loved. Ye'll wake each morning snuggled up to a hard cock that'll see to your needs. Ye'll never want in that area. Real men, good men, provide for their wives in all ways. A wife who enjoys the marriage bed makes for a better wife. It is up to her husbands to see that she does."

Something in his words woke feelings she'd long thought dead. Her mind, her soul, and her nethers felt as though a whirlwind swirled inside and all around her. The air around her was charged like it was when a twister was in the offing. Goosebumps raised all along her skin, but not from the cold.

"Bullshit! You don't believe that any more than I do."

Gavan shook his head again, unbuttoned the cuffs on his shirt sleeves, and began to roll them up, revealing strong, tanned arms covered with black hair. She was transfixed; she couldn't look away. He pulled a gold pocket watch out of his trousers and checked the time.

"I guess we'd better get on with this. I'll nay indulge yer temper. Yer going to learn from the get-go just who calls the shots and who gets her bottom spanked."

Elizabeth picked up the empty bucket in the corner of the cell and swung it at him, only barely missing him.

"You come near me, and I'll scream," she threatened.

Gavan chuckled. "I suspect ye will. Most lasses caterwaul something awful when their getting their hide tanned. I mean to put a sting in your tail that will last a day or two."

She was trying to circle around him, but misjudged how quickly he could move.

He was a big man but moved with the power and grace of a large, lethal wildcat. He closed the distance between them, seizing her hair in his fist as she tried to dart past him. Gavan used her inertia to swing her back toward the little cot where he took a seat, stripped her pants and bloomers down to her knees and tipped her over his hard thigh, using the other to trap her legs between his.

The air was cool on her exposed backside, but the

place between her legs was hotter than a blacksmith's forge. The idea of that man having his hands on her bare skin made her catch her breath; the buds of her breasts beaded, and her core begin to pulse in a way it never had before. She prayed he wouldn't be able to tell how desperately she wanted him to make the ache and the fear go away.

Elizabeth found herself summarily upended in a position misbehaving women had been finding themselves since the beginning of time, although, it was a first for her. She wriggled in an attempt to get away but failed.

Before she could do more than that, Gavan's strong hand pinned her down while the other collided with her naked flesh.

Elizabeth yowled from the intensity of the pain that radiated across her backside.

Gavan began to spank her, rhythmically, and with a great deal of strength. She could not believe he, or anyone else for that matter, was doing this to her. Gavan covered her backside with blow after stinging blow.

Elizabeth bit her lip to try to keep from crying. She was determined this brute would not get the better of her. The worst part was that all those lovely, tingly butterflies in her belly that erupted each time he was near took flight. She feared that, even worse than the physical pain from the spanking, was the very real possibility that the honey that now pooled in her most feminine place would begin to leak and drip down onto his leg. Her mortification from her arousal was far worse than the pain he was inflicting on her backside.

His hand landed targeted swats to her behind before working its way down to the juncture of her bottom and her legs. Gavan delivered several well-aimed smacks to that sensitive spot, which produced a howl in response before he continued down and punished the backs of her thighs as well.

"You bastard!" she wailed.

"Nay, lass, that's not the way to convince yer husband he's gotten through to ye and ye mean to behave."

All she wanted was for him to stop. She needed him to stop. It hurt. And, if he didn't stop soon, he might notice the effect his spanking was having on her. She was not unaware of the parts of a man's body and how they reacted when they wanted a woman. She could feel his erection building beneath her. It felt far larger than any she had caught a glimpse of over the years. It seemed to pound in the same rhythm as the hand that was blistering her arse.

Elizabeth thought a man's member was a fearsome thing when aroused, large and hard and jutting out from his body, the veining in stark relief to the stretched and taught skin. But she also found them fascinating. Sometimes at night, when she could hear her men fucking, she wondered what it might be like to touch one, what it would be like to be mounted and have it thrust in and out. What was it like to be possessed by a man and have him stroke her private sheath with his engorged staff? Did her longing mean she was the whore the sheriff had sought to make her? Had he, somehow, sensed the wantonness of her thoughts? And what of the man who was inflicting blow after blow on her delicate

31

backside; could he sense the desire that raged within her?

Gavan's spanking hurt, but there was something that felt right about being face down over his knee, his hand smacking her ass at the same tempo as his cock throbbed beneath her. Elizabeth was so confused; how could it hurt so much and still have the power to arouse and entice her? His powerful arm kept her pinned in place as his hand descended over and over, landing repeated blows to her backside.

She wriggled on his lap, not certain if it was to get away, or to get him to do something she didn't completely understand. She wailed in pain and outrage, but Gavan continued to deliver the spanking he seemed determined to inflict.

"I hate you. I'm going to kill you, asshole; fuck you!"

"Ye'll do no such thing, lass, at least, not the killing part. The fucking part ye'll be doing a lot of. Yer going to have to learn to behave."

He punctuated each word with a hard swat to her behind, which she was quite sure was red and swollen.

"I'm not going to be your wife, you motherfucker."

"Nay, lass, ye'll be whatever I tell ye that ye are, and I say ye will be my wife and will learn to mind."

Her ass was absolutely on fire; it hurt, and Gavan seemed in no hurry to stop. Repeatedly, he struck her bottom. She lost control and began to wail in desperation. She twisted and turned but could not get away from him. He held her in place sprawled over his lap and calmly lectured her on her language while he continued to wallop her behind. Once the tears had started, they quickly devolved into great heaving sobs.

"Please, stop. Stop! Please! I'll do what you want. Just don't hit me anymore."

Gavan's hand came down lightly and rested on her sore buttocks before he began rubbing soothing circles over her heated flesh. Part of her wanted nothing more than to get away from him, but a growing part wanted to embrace the comfort he was offering. His hand continued to caress her.

She moaned and swore she heard him softly chuckle. One of his hands rubbed the small of her back and stroked her spine. He used the other, the one that had so easily brought her to tears, to trail down from her punished globes to between her legs.

"Spread yer legs for me, lass," he crooned.

"No," she whispered, never wanting, or fearing, anything more in her life.

He swatted her backside. "You didna tell me no, Lizzie. Now, do as yer told, and let me offer ye a little comfort and pleasure."

Gavan nudged her upper thighs, and she parted them. He slipped his hand between her legs and explored the warmth he found there. Elizabeth mewled in quiet protest, but his answering growl silenced and soothed her almost immediately.

"Good girl. Ye best get used to the feeling of yer man's hands on yer body. Yer a beautiful woman, Lizzie. Ye will be well and truly loved."

He reached further between her legs and found her swollen nub. His fingers surrounded it, tugging gently.

Elizabeth gasped as a jolt of pure awakening shot through her system. She had pleasured herself in the past, but it had never felt like this. She could feel her channel pulsing with a life force she had never felt. The more he focused his attention on that bit of bundled nerves, the more erratic and labored her breathing became.

Elizabeth felt a wave of warmth rise up from the nerve center he was manipulating. It rose from the actual spot Gavan fondled, to her belly and on up to her swollen nipples. The tremors of pleasure intensified as she neared the edge of completion that had always frightened her. She tried to pull back from the brink of the unknown... the unknown that had always frightened her and yet had beckoned her. Gavan intensified the stimulation he was providing. Elizabeth realized she would be unable to stop herself from tumbling over the edge into that abyss of feeling and desire. Clasping his leg, Elizabeth let go of the last remnants of her control and screamed in hedonistic, and unfamiliar, abandon.

As she slipped over the edge, a groundswell of pure pleasure washed over her. She surrendered to the sensation and felt as though her spirit had separated from her body and was set free. The surge that enveloped her was powerful and resulted in an enormous feeling of bliss that caused her to almost black out.

"There, now, isn't that better?" he asked, gently stroking her from the little nub to the entrance to her core. "The sheriff and his wife are going to witness our vows and the judge will perform the ceremony. Do ye think ye can be a good girl and behave?"

She nodded. She didn't want to comply but, more than that, she wanted to hear him call her a good girl as he soothed her heated globes.

"All right, then, we'll be done with it," his leg released hers, and he helped her to her feet, tugging up her undergarments and bringing her to sit on his lap.

He withdrew a white linen handkerchief from his pocket and used it to dry her tears. Elizabeth couldn't remember a time anyone had cared enough to do that. He hugged her briefly before allowing her to get up then pressed a chaste kiss to her temple.

"It'll be all right, Lizzie, ye'll see."

As if on cue, the sheriff, his wife, and the judge joined them.

Gavan took her hand in his, and they faced the judge.

The judge began to speak about marriage and its promises and duties.

Elizabeth found herself focusing on anything other than what was being said until he asked Gavan to take his vows.

"I, Gavan MacLean, take thee, Elizabeth Morgan, to be my wedded wife, to have and to hold ..."

Then, she tuned him out as well.

The judge turned to her, as did the eyes of all the others crowded into her small cell.

"Do you," intoned the judge, "Elizabeth Morgan, take Gavan MacLean to be your wedded husband, to have and to hold from this day forward, for better, for worse, for richer, for poorer, in sickness and in health, to love, honor, and obey until death do you part and according to God's holy ordinance?"

Elizabeth could feel their eyes boring holes into her soul. Would it be so wrong to just let them hang her and be done with it? What did she know about this man, other that his hands could deliver pain and pleasure in equal measure?

"Lizzie, ye need to say I do," Gavan prompted her.

She said nothing, trying to see if there was any way out, any way to escape. A hard swat to her rump jolted her from her internal musings.

"Shit! That hurts," she snarled at Gavan.

"Aye, lass, it was supposed to. Now, ye either take yer vows, or I'll put ye back over my knee and ye'll take them as I paddle yer backside to an even deeper shade of red. Now, Lizzie," he growled.

"Why? Why do you want to marry me?"

"Because yer the most important thing to me. This is the only way to keep ye alive. Ye needn't fear, lass, ye'll be well cared for," Gavan said, keeping his voice even.

"Like you took care of me when you beat my ass?" she hissed. "Like when you took liberties with me before we were wed?"

"That's enough, Lizzie. I warned ye if ye didn't agree to behave and agree to take yer vows, I'd spank ye, which is what I did. All I did after that was to offer ye a little comfort, which ye seemed to greatly enjoy. Now, ye either say 'I do,' or I'll put ye back over my knee, and ye'll answer properly in short order."

"I'm waiting for your answer, Elizabeth," said the judge.

She scanned the faces of those who surrounded her; there was no sympathy there. Gavan's grip on her arm

36

reminded her there was no escape. Delaying the inevitable would do nothing more than get her spanked again. But her chance of escape would present itself, and she'd be ready.

"As I seem to have no choice, I do," she said, bitterly.

Gavan placed a simple silver wedding band with an intricate design and three gemstones on her finger before placing a simple band with the same design on his own.

"Then, by the powers vested in me, I pronounce you man and wife," said the judge. "Try to be happy, Elizabeth, I believe this man cares for you."

Elizabeth snorted. "What you believe is that you won't have to feel guilty for killing the daughter of your dead best friend, the daughter who you never once lifted so much as a finger to help."

Gavan's response was quick, painful, and set her up on her tiptoes. "Enough, Lizzie. Ye behave. The judge saved yer life. Now, apologize for showing him the sharp side of yer tongue."

When she hesitated, he swatted her again.

"Fine. I apologize."

Gavan shook his head. "Ye'd best get it through yer head that yer going to mind me, else it will be a long and painful ride home for ye." Gavan turned to the judge. "I promised ye, Lizzie and I would be gone tonight, and I think we need to head out."

The sheriff had left her cell but returned with a set of manacles and what appeared to be a sharpening strap for a man's razor.

"I think you might need these," he said handing both to Gavan.

Her new husband tucked both into the saddle bags he had tossed over his shoulder and led her to the livery stable, where he swung up on his big Appaloosa.

Another man, the fair one from the trial, the one who seemed to be her new husband's opposite and opposing force, held a buckskin and a bay packhorse. The other man handed her a parcel.

Her husband quirked an eyebrow at him.

"She isn't going to wear trousers. Those are meant for a man, and she's anything but manly," he answered the unverbalized question. "Ye know, as well as I do, that every man in that courtroom was looking at her feminine bits."

"Ye have to admit, her feminine bits are enchanting, so ye canna blame them."

"Aye, but she's ours now, and I'll nay have other men coveting what's ours."

Gavan laughed. "Are ye daff? Just because you put a skirt over it doesn't mean men aren't going to look and imagine themselves between her thighs."

Elizabeth tried to punch him, and he, once again, used her own inertia to redirect her energy and landed several more swats on her bottom, making her dance.

"Enough, Lizzie. Yer a beautiful woman, and some men are always thinking about getting between a pretty girl's legs."

"Only some?" Elizabeth asked, sarcastically.

Gavan smacked her backside again. "I said enough, Lizzie. Ye watch yer mouth, lass, or I'll find some soap and water to wash it out for ye. And, aye, some. Men like

Caelan and me, once we're wed, we no longer look at any other woman. But we'll look at you plenty."

"Aye," started the fair-haired man, "and we'll do more than look and imagine. We'll be the ones who spend a fair amount of time there fucking yer cunny and yer arse to our heart's content."

"Caelan bought these for ye, Lizzie, go into that stall and get changed."

"I won't."

"Ye will, or ye'll get another spanking and ride to our camp in yer chemise and bloomers. Cae is right, ye'll nay wear trousers anymore."

Elizabeth snatched the parcel and stomped to the far back stall, followed by the man she now knew as Caelan. Entering the stall, she whirled on him. "What the hell do you think you're doing?"

"Gavan's had his hands on yer naked backside, I think it's only fair I get a look at ye, as well."

"Arrrgggghhh!" She snarled, turning her back and changing her clothes.

He held out his hand to her.

She flung the trousers in his face.

Like Gavan, he reacted surprisingly fast and in a similar way. He bent her over his thigh and walloped her behind several times.

"Settle down, Lizzie, or ye'll need more pillows than we have to cushion yer bottom when Gavan takes yer maidenhead."

He folded the trousers over the stall door, took hold of her upper arm, and led her back to the main portion of the stables where Gavan waited, already seated on his horse.

"Yer right, Gav, she's got a bountiful arse for spanking. I can only imagine what it'll be like to fuck. Good thing that, once we're back at home, I won't have to imagine it." He took Elizabeth over to Gavan, grasped her around the waist, and handed her up to him. "Up ye get."

She struggled and wiggled. The feel of his male member hardening caused a momentary bout of panic, causing her to wriggle and squirm.

"Enough, Lizzie. Either ye ride in front of me sitting in my lap, or face down across it."

She said nothing but settled.

The other man mounted the buckskin and, picking up the lead of the bay, headed out.

As they rode, Gavan began to unbutton the buttons of her shirt. When she slapped at his hands, he produced a small length of rope and simply bound them behind her back.

"I'll bet she has beautiful tits," said Caelan, watching with keen interest as Gavan opened her shirt, unlaced her corset, and pulled her chemise out of the way.

"You can't," she hissed. "Not in front of him."

Both men chuckled.

"Ye'll find, lass, there's very little either of us does to ye, that the other isn't witness to." He gasped as her bosom sprang free and reached across the distance to trace the area around her nipple that was of a darker hue than the rest of her skin. "So beautiful," he said in a reverent tone.

"Aye," said Gavan, huskily, and gathered the hem of

her skirt, tucking it into her waist band. As bloomers were not fully enclosed, he had no trouble revealing the mahogany hair at the apex of her thighs, or exposing the nub that resided there.

"Ach, would ye look at her clit? God, it looks to be begging to be sucked."

Gavan nodded. "Aye, our Lizzie is a sight to behold. I canna waiting to get between her legs and breach her maidenhead while ye hold her still for me."

"That's monstrous!" she cried.

"Nay, lass. 'Tis our way. Gavan will be the one to actually breach your maidenhead, but I will hold ye and add to yer pleasure. We'll see ye well pleasured this night... and for the rest of yer days. It's important to both of us that ye be happy."

He reached out and touched her.

Her response was a sharp inhalation of breath and bucking wildly on Gavan's lap as Caelan fingered her much as Gavan had done earlier. As much as she didn't want it to, she had to admit it felt wonderful. She closed her eyes.

"Ye will watch him pleasure ye, Lizzie. Open yer eyes."

She didn't want to, but she did. She couldn't help but watch. She watched as he circled her clit with his fingertips and played with her wet lips, gently tracing the entrance to her core. Elizabeth wondered at her own wanton response to his bold caresses.

After a few moments, Gavan untied her hands and allowed her to arrange her clothing.

3

ELIZABETH

"I HADN'T EXPECTED ye to be gone all afternoon," said Gavan to his partner.

"Well, while you were persuading our bride to take her vows, I was trying to make tonight a bit easier on the lass. I don't know about ye, but I intend to see our marriage consummated before the sunrise."

"What do you mean 'our bride'?" Elizabeth asked, remembering something Gavan had said before they were wed.

Caelan chuckled. "I wondered if he'd shared that information with ye. To tell the truth, Lizzie, ye've now got not just one husband, but two. When ye took yer vows to Gavan, they applied to me, as well."

"Who are you?"

"Lizzie, this is Caelan MacAllister, yer other husband. I mentioned him briefly right before I had to spank ye."

"Gavan, did ye really have to spank her?"

"Aye. She had no intention of behaving, and she needs to learn to mind. She's got a glorious arse, Cae, round and firm and a beautiful ivory."

"Hmm. Well, ye could have waited until I was there."

Gavan laughed, and the other man grinned before continuing, "Our Lizzie is a naughty thing. I suspect ye'll see me paddle her quite often, and will probably have to do so, yerself. She's nay of the mind to be a sweet and biddable bride, are ye, Lizzie? The judge performed the one legally binding ceremony between you and me. But you are bound just as tightly to Caelan as ye are to me. If you are married to one of us, ye are married to the other, as well."

Caelan held up his hand, "See? I have a matching wedding band."

She shook her head, her hair spilling down around her shoulders. "No. No. That isn't done. Did the judge know about this?" she asked, blushing, as Gavan's words about her being shared between them came back to her.

"He knows he married you to Gavan to keep you from the hangman's noose. But, at our home in Bridgewater, all of the women share at least two husbands. Ye'll be no different."

"It'll be fine, Lizzie," said Gavan before turning to his partner. "Caelan, after she acquiesced, I gave her a bit of pleasure to help settle her. Once she came, she was a lot more amenable."

"Aren't they always?" chuckled Caelan.

"I know we agreed that I would breach her maidenhead, but I think it's only right that you prepare her for that. She was drenched by the time I slipped my hand between her legs."

Elizabeth felt her entire body flushing with embarrassment, and something more. She'd never thought of herself as a prude, but these two men were riding along, discussing what sounded like their plan to share her tonight. She had to admit the thought of being with either one of them had a certain appeal, but both of them? That was just wrong.

They rode into a small box canyon that Elizabeth had used to hide stolen herds several times. It was well-hidden, had plenty of water and forage, and was easily defendable. A large campfire had been set up, as well as a temporary corral for the horses. Spanning the width between two trees and close to the running stream was a canvas of some sort that had been strung up to form a canopy. What worried Elizabeth was that, beneath it, there was only one, exceptionally large bedroll.

They brought the horses to a stop, and Caelan stepped off his horse and handed its reins, as well as the bay's, to Gavan. He pulled her gently from in front of Gavan, who rode over to the corral to unsaddle and make the horses ready for the night.

Elizabeth struggled when Caelan held her tight against his chest, his member poking at her through his trousers.

"Easy, Lizzie. It'll be all right. Ye have two husbands who care for ye now. Two men to love, honor, and cherish ye. Gavan says yer a passionate lass. Given how ye responded to being spanked and then finger-fucked, I think ye'll find having two husbands to keep ye warm and satisfied will suit ye just fine."

"No, it isn't right..."

"Who's to say what is right? When we were in the war, we lived for a while in Mohamir, where this kind of marriage is commonplace. They believe, as do Gavan and I, that a woman with two husbands is far less likely to fall on hard times. Gavan's sister became a widow, and she was forced to marry a man she didna love to provide for herself and her children. We will keep ye from that. If one of us is killed, the other will provide for ye and our children."

Elizabeth thought he made it sound perfectly logical.

"How will you know whose children are whose?" she whispered, trying to tap down the desire that was pooling below her belly and across her nipples, beading in response to his words and his hands that softly caressed her body.

"Who the actual sire is? It won't matter. As yer are our bride, the children will belong to all of us."

Gavan had finished with the horses and returned to Elizabeth and Caelan. Without removing her from Caelan's embrace, he added his own wandering hands to her body, feeling the weight of her breasts.

He bent down and whispered, "I love ye, Lizzie. I know ye probably didna believe that, but it's true. We wanted to break ye out every evening when they took ye to jail so we could protect ye. But ye'd have had a death sentence hanging over yer head."

"So we waited," continued Caelan. "But, had the

judge not agreed to Gavan's plan, we would have seen ye freed, even gone to Canada, if we'd had to. We never would have let them hang ye. Yer our wife now and, like Gavan, I pledge ye my heart and all that I am."

Elizabeth wasn't sure when she had stopped trying to get away and just began to respond to their fondling, which continued to grow bolder. Caelan pressed himself into the cleft between her butt cheeks, and she could feel Gavan's hard length pulsing on her belly. Their whispering warmed her skin. The sensual feel of their hands acting in concert fired her blood and she moaned.

"We have a beautiful bride, Caelan. I've only seen her naked bottom, but it was fair beyond belief."

His lips nibbled and kissed along her jawline, barely passing over her lips before starting down the column of her neck. Gavan pressed his lower body against her mons as he brought his hands up to squeeze her breasts, lightly pinching her nipples.

"I think, Gavan, our bride has on too many clothes," Caelan said, nuzzling the nape of her neck.

Between the two of them and the sensual web they were weaving, Elizabeth felt on fire. Her nipples were now hard enough that they pressed against the whalebone corset and bordered on painful, and her feminine sheath pulsed in a way it never had, and it seemed to coincide with the throbbing of both of their cocks.

Caelan held her close, his hands spanning her hips and holding her in close contact with his staff. As one hand left her hip, it travelled down between her and

Gavan's pulsing rod. He covered her mons, cupping it and pulling her into even tighter proximity to his groin.

Gavan reached up to the neck of her shirt and began unbuttoning it.

When she tried to raise her hands up to ward him off, she found her arms were pinned down and back by Caelan.

The two worked together to remove her shirt and then her corset.

"We need to get ye out of that corset, Lizzie," said Caelan.

Reaching being his back, Gavan pulled out a large Bowie knife and showed it to her. For the first time, fear was in competition with lust as her overriding emotion. Did he mean to kill her? Had he saved her from the hangman just to cut her up?

Gavan spun her around in Caelan's arms. Placing the tip under the laces, he brought it up, neatly slicing through them much like a hot knife would slice butter. The corset fell to the ground. In that instance, she felt exposed, even though she still had on her chemise and bloomers. Her breasts fell free; their shape and size clearly visible, even though they were covered with a thin cloth.

Gavan turned her back around and smiled appreciatively at her curves.

The butterflies that had taken flight in her belly moved down, and their wings fanned the flames of her desire. Her nipples were puckered from the cool night air, but the space between her legs was a raging inferno.

Gavan ran his hands down the front of her body. He

dropped to one knee; his hands came up to her waist, pulling at the skirt and petticoat, dragging them down past her hips.

She shivered everywhere she felt the touch of his hand, or his breath.

He couldn't seem to stop staring at her tits, and the place where her legs joined her body, as if he knew how damp her sex had become and how it pulsed with need. He skimmed his hands farther down, removing her long socks and boots, leaving her clad in only her chemise and bloomers.

"Our bride is getting more and more aroused." Gavan said, sliding his hand inside the waistband of her bloomers before combing his fingers through the silky curls at the apex of her thighs and parting her swollen lips before just circling the entrance of her core and stroking lightly. "The lass is soaked, Caelan. I think it's yer turn to get her naked and see our bride in all her glory."

Elizabeth's knees began to buckle as they turned her around so that she was now held captive in Gavan's embrace. Caelan leaned down, sliding her bloomers past her rump, down her thighs and calves, before removing them completely, tracing his fingers along the inside of her thigh. His hand cupped the silky triangle while his finger began to strum across the distended nub it found there.

She moaned and would have fallen forward if Gavan had not kept her erect.

She shook her head. "No," she barely managed to sigh.

"Aye, lass. There's nothing to fear, or be ashamed of.

We're yer husbands, and we're going to claim ye tonight as our bride. Both of us. All of our clothes will come off so we can see each other as God intended us to. Then, we'll lay down in the nice soft bed I made. I'll make ye ready for Gavan, much like he did earlier after he spanked ye. Only, when I'm done, Gavan will get between yer thighs and breach yer maidenhead. When he's finished pleasuring ye and left ye full of his seed, I'll put ye on yer belly and take ye like a stallion takes his mare and do the same. Ye'll know only the brief pain of Gavan tearing yer maidenhead but, then, we'll only give ye pleasure."

Elizabeth's breathing was shallow and erratic. His words inflamed her lustful thoughts. She had always thought she was wanton, as she longed to feel the most intimate caress of a man. His words were seductive and, slowly, she began to want not just one, but both of them to have carnal knowledge of her body. She could no longer form thoughts, much less words, on her own. All that existed for her was being held between two strong, virile, highly aroused men. Her pussy throbbed, and she moaned deeply when Caelan slipped her chemise off so that she was finally naked.

He wrapped his arms around her as Gavan released her.

Gavan went into the lean-to and removed his clothing. He turned to face her, unashamed of his body and its response to her proximity and nudity. It wasn't the first time Elizabeth had seen a cock, but never had she seen one that was so long and thick. It seemed to deny the laws of nature, standing straight out from his body. It was suspended and bobbed in anticipation; the thought of what it was anticipating thrilled and frightened her at the same time. He couldn't expect that thing to fit up inside her, could he?

"Do ye like the look of Gavan's naked body, Lizzie?" whispered Caelan. "Do ye see his cock? Do ye want him to fuck ye with it? I can't wait to see it disappear into that sweet cunny of yours. Even better will be when I watch my own sink into your wet heat. Do ye see how finely he's made? We will both worship ye with our bodies until we have ye exhausted, but well-fucked and happy. Can ye feel my cock straining to get out, Lizzie? We've waited for ye a long time, and will spend the rest of our lives taking care of all yer needs."

Elizabeth watched Gavan approach. His naked body was covered in slabbed and corded muscles with dark hair covering his extremities, chest and nested around his engorged member.

"Here, Cae," said Gavan in a husky voice. "Let me have her while ye get naked."

Caelan had no more released his hold than Gavan swept her up in his arms. His chest hair was coarse and tickled her skin. He strode to the improvised bed, kneeling down and propping himself against a makeshift headboard that Caelan had constructed. Gavan pulled her between his legs, cradling her thighs between his own. The feel of his skin next to hers was a new experience yet, somehow, it felt familiar and right. He reached around and began gently kneading her breasts.

She moaned.

Caelan quickly shucked out of his clothes and stopped to poke the fire before coming to join them. Like

Gavan, he was tall and well-built. He had less body hair, and it was a fair gingery color. His cock might not have been quite as long, but it was easily as thick, and hard. A clear fluid dripped from the tip.

"Ye see that, Lizzie?" Gavan whispered into her ear, continuing to fondle her breasts, tracing the dusky center pieces, strumming his thumbs across her nipples before giving them a pinch and then a tug. "Between how hard he is and his seed leaking from the head of his cock, that's how ye know Caelan wants ye as bad as I. Can ye feel my cock nestled between yer globes? Can ye feel my need for ye, Lizzie?"

She nodded and moaned, in the grip of a demand and desire for something she was only beginning to comprehend. Her eyes were riveted to Caelan's approach, his mighty staff primed for use, but she couldn't focus on that. Gavan's hands were far too distracting, as were his whispered words, some of which she didn't understand.

Caelan lay down beside her, stroking the inside of her thigh before leaning over to swirl his tongue in her bellybutton. Elizabeth's pussy spasmed as Caelan inhaled, taking in her scent. He eased himself between her legs, reaching up her body. His fingers closed around her nipples, giving them both a squeeze, which tightened to a pinch. One hand slipped down between her thighs, where he played briefly with her swollen nub before trailing down her slit to the opening of her core, barely penetrating her there. He probed it gently and shallowly.

"Aye, Gav, her maidenhead's intact."

He gathered some of her honied essence before

bringing his fingers back up to his mouth and licking them clean.

Elizabeth couldn't stifle the moan, or the pulsing of her core.

"Open," he whispered as he slid his fingers along her lips, before slipping them into her mouth.

"That's it," crooned Gavan, "suck his fingers clean."

Caelan continued to play with her nipples, first one and then the other, twisting, pulling, tugging, and pinching. He pushed his fingers a bit deeper into her mouth. The taste of her own honey on Caelan's fingertips was as intoxicating as moonshine and, with everything they were doing and saying, she felt a bit tipsy.

"For now, ye'll suck our fingers when we feed ye yer honey, or our cream, but ye'll learn to suck our cocks. So many things for our bonny lass to learn. Ye want to please us, don't ye, Lizzie?" murmured Gavan.

"Such a good girl," added Caelan as he withdrew his fingers from her mouth and trailed them down her chin, throat, and between the valley of her breasts.

Caelan blew kisses down her body, worshiping her with his lips and tongue. When he latched onto her nipple, Elizabeth's body arched up, and she cried out in wonder and delight. She swore she could feel his suckling, not just on her pebbled peak, but down in the throbbing nubbin at the juncture of her thighs and her pussy beyond.

He inched down her body, whispering kisses, licking and sucking as he went. He parted her thighs, lifting a leg over each shoulder, placing her molten core right in his face. She tried to close her legs, but he had himself wedged between them. She knew the tissue around her opening was slick and swollen from arousal. Caelan lightly stroked a finger across it. He lowered his head, nuzzling her pussy.

She heard a whimper and realized it was coming from her. She wasn't in pain. She'd never felt like this, so alive and connected to all things—but mostly to these two men... her husbands. The little pearl between her legs was practically throbbing.

Caelan nipped it before latching on and sucking.

Elizabeth tried to arch her body up but was held firmly in place by Gavan. Her legs stayed in place, but her body trembled all over.

Caelan looked up at her before slowly, deliberately lowering his mouth to her. She could feel his heat, feel his breath. He sucked in her small nubbin, suckling for a moment before trailing his tongue down to her virgin sheath. His tongue slid around, gathering every bit of her honey that had dribbled out. He drove his tongue up inside her, and the fireworks that Gavan had produced back in the jail cell returned, brighter than the Fourth of July.

Looking past her to Gavan, he said, "She's well primed, Gav. She's slick from the honey she's already produced. I don't know about you, but I'm near to dying with the want of her."

"Aye, Cae. Let's switch places for a bit, while I make her ours first and, then, ye can ease your need in her sweet cunny. Can't he, love?"

Elizabeth couldn't speak, only nod.

Gavan gently swapped places with Caelan, who lay

back against the pillows before bringing her to rest against his chest. Elizabeth felt a little like a sacrifice to some ancient god, naked and spread out before them, but she also felt her own power. These two strong, virile men wanted her to be their bride, wanted to share a life with her. An unconventional one, no doubt, but, still, Caelan had said they would never have let her hang and, instinctively, she knew it to be true.

The only thing in life that mattered now was pleasing these men, her husbands, so they would continue this delicious torture. She may have been unsure or even reluctant when they started, but now she knew she was made for them—as they had been made for her. Her body trembled as Gavan stroked her. The quivering became shaking as she lost touch with any reality other than the one they had created.

She needed, *wanted*, more. Reaching up to cup Gavan's head with one hand, she reached back to touch Caelan, as well, and felt his fingers lace through hers as he brought them up to kiss them. She brought Caelan's hand down and clasped it to her breast, crying out when Gavan nipped the distended tip, refocusing her on him.

He latched on tightly as he flicked his tongue against it.

Elizabeth wriggled and squirmed, not to get away, but to draw him closer and encourage a more intimate touch. Their combined groaning emboldened and enraptured her. Placing her hand over his as Gavan stroked her; she encouraged him to do so more deeply and purred in cat-like satisfaction when he did.

Elizabeth bowed her back, shoving her mons against

his hand. Her body shuddered in ecstasy as every synapse fired and pleasure exploded throughout her body. Never had anything felt so right and so marvelous. She had never believed that Paradise existed on Earth, but now believed it was to be had and embraced. His hardened length lay trapped between them, and her sheath pulsed in the same rhythm as his shaft.

"Gavan," she cried in wondered rapture, clinging to him with one hand and squeezing Caelan's thigh with the other.

Gavan removed his hand from between her legs as he rolled more fully on top of her.

Elizabeth realized he meant now to take her virginity. She struggled, momentarily frightened until she heard Caelan at her back, nuzzling her neck and nipping at her ear lobe, whispering words of love, sex, and encouragement. Still, Elizabeth tried to move from underneath him.

"Nay, lass." Gavan crooned. "Ye didna want to deny me. I am yer husband, and 'tis my right to claim ye. It'll be all right, Lizzie, give yourself to me, to us. Let us show you what it is to be well and truly loved. Ye want this, don't ye, Lizzie?"

She nodded and knew it was true. If this made her a wanton, then a wanton was what she wanted to be.

Before she could change her mind, Gavan's mouth descended, capturing hers, his tongue beginning a seductive dance within.

She squirmed beneath him, not sure if she wanted what was to come, knowing there was no retreat and that she didn't truly want one.

He settled himself more firmly between her thighs.

Caelan reached between them and caught some of the slick wet that her earlier orgasm had produced in abundance. He brought it up and rubbed her clit in circular motions, rumbling to her as she felt the head of Gavan's staff probing for the entrance to her wet heat.

Elizabeth mewled in need. The ticklish sensations began all over again but, this time, she burned like a wildfire had been lit within her and now raced out of control throughout her entire being.

Gavan kissed her relentlessly, making it difficult to focus on anything other than pleasing him and listening to every fiber of her being that cried out for him to claim her fully. She let him slip his hands underneath her, his palms gripping her hips while his fingers gently held her buttocks. She grimaced slightly from the residual effects of the spanking he'd given her before their wedding.

She looked to see him staring at her intently. "Yay or nay, Lizzie?"

She nodded. Steadying her, he kissed her passionately as he drove his cock powerfully up into her, stretching her entrance, shattering the delicate tissue that had kept her a maid, and seating himself fully within her.

Elizabeth screamed into his mouth. She was unprepared for the pain that erupted as he destroyed her maidenhead.

He whispered kisses over her face and nuzzled her neck.

She held her breath, waiting for something, but she wasn't quite sure what.

He gave her only a moment to catch her breath and

for her tightness to soften and accept his penetration. Then, slowly, he began to stroke her with long, slow thrusts that quickly turned the pain into pleasure as her body received and then accepted his dominant possession. Her sheath hugged his cock; he groaned and then rumbled his carnal need for her as he picked up the pace of his plunging rod.

Gavan held her tightly to him as he rolled his hips, moving his cock deeper and faster in her pussy. She could feel every inch and texture of his large staff as it grazed her vaginal walls. She thought she would never forget the incredible way it felt and filled her. There was another gradual building of sensual pleasure as Elizabeth's body responded fully to his claiming. It swirled around her swollen nub and spread down and through to her heated sheath as he continued to drive within her. She could feel an almost overwhelming trembling in her nether regions as it expanded and spread throughout her body.

His movements became more deliberate and forceful. The faster he moved, the larger he seemed to grow within her. Her muscles tensed in a way she now knew was the precursor to her own climax.

Gavan's lips moved down the side of her neck to the base of her throat.

As her muscles convulsed in a powerful orgasm, she felt his seed begin to flood her womb. Elizabeth screamed again, but wasn't sure if it was in pleasure, or abject surrender. Her pussy shuddered blissfully all up and down his length as he continued to send his essence to the very end of her channel.

When he was finally still, he kissed her before rolling from atop her body and stroking the inside of her upper thigh in a manner that was comforting, yet possessive. She could feel the mingled essence of their coupling drying there, as well as in the soft hair covering her mons.

"Good girl. Ye have so much pleasure to look forward to. We'll see to it. We're going to start plugging yer bottom hole so that, in time, we can share you at the same time instead of taking turns. While Gavan fucks your sweet pussy, I'll take your arse," Caelan whispered in her ear.

Elizabeth shuddered at the thought but had neither the will, nor the ability, to do anything other than allow him to continue to stroke her body soothingly.

Gavan gently lifted her body off of Caelan's, taking his place and settling her back against him, cupping her breasts and lightly rubbing her nipples. The sensitized tips responded by pebbling up and beginning to ache.

"Good girl, Lizzie," Gavan crooned. "See how responsive our beautiful bride is, Cae? Even after losing her maidenhead, she hungers for more; don't ye, Lizzie?"

"No," she whispered, truly frightened that she was some kind of wanton.

"Nay, lass. Yer body doesn't lie. Die ye not find pleasure with what Gavan did?"

She nodded.

"There's nothing wrong with that, Lizzie. If yer husbands pleasure ye more often than themselves, then they've done right by ye. And I did do right be ye, didn't I?"

Again, she nodded.

"And ye liked when I readied ye for Gavan didn't ye? Ye felt pleasure from my touch?"

"Yes," she said, finally finding her voice.

"Then would ye deny Caelan the same pleasure ye gave to me and that ye felt yerself?" Gavan crooned.

She shook her head.

"Then tell him, Lizzie. Tell him ye want him to make ye his as well. Go on, lass, say it. Tell Caelan ye want to feel his cock deep inside ye, stroking ye before he gives ye his seed."

She looked down at Caelan who seemed anxious but was willing to be patient with her. The fact was she did want to feel him inside her sheath, thrusting in and out until he emptied himself."

"Yes," she nodded. "I want to feel Caelan as well."

Caelan kissed her, slowly and deeply exploring the recesses of her mouth, enticing her tongue to come and dance with his, savoring the kiss and the time he was taking as it was the only thing important thing to him. She was beginning to believe that her pleasure was at least as important to them as their own... if not more.

From the time she'd started developing her womanly figure, her dreams had been filled with images of men doing the kinds of things to her she had seen men doing to their women. She had been intrigued from a young age about what went on between men and women. She questioned whether or not the shudder she had made in response to Caelan's words was one of revulsion, or arousal. She had been told not to, and repeatedly beaten, at the orphanage for exploring her body and finding pleasure in the act. The refrain of having a wanton nature, being no more than a lustful slut and not welcome in polite society ran through her head.

Maybe they had all been right. She had laid in one man's arms while another took her virginity. Gavan and Caelan were re-positioning her so that Caelan could make her his wife, as well as Gavan's and, instead of being repulsed by the idea, she welcomed it.

"Nay, lass. Tis nothing to fear or be ashamed of," murmured Caelan. "It only shows us what ye like, that you have an endless depth of passion, and that Gavan well pleased ye. Now, let's see if I can do the same."

Caelan lifted her away from Gavan and placed her between them so that she was lying prone against Gavan's body. She wondered how a man as solidly built could be comfortable when she was lying on him. Caelan's hand rested on the small of her back and stroked downward, his finger trailing between her twin globes past her pussy as it sought the turgid nub between her legs that he had rubbed and tugged previously.

Elizabeth caught her breath from the pleasurable sensations radiating out from the small button to her core. She could feel the beginnings of another powerful climax.

Caelan removed his hand and swatted her swollen vulva lightly before putting his hand back between her legs to soothe the slight sting. It didn't really hurt, but seemed to inflame the entire region, and she squirmed. This time, he probed the opening of her core, delicately slipping a single digit into her cunt.

Caelan chuckled, the sound full of genuine amusement. He continued to delve within, and she squirmed and writhed, lying atop Gavan, trying to rub her sensitized nub along the hardened length she could feel trying to rise again.

He removed his finger and leaned close to whisper, "Do ye wish to have yer second husband breach your cunny with his cock?"

"Yes, please..."

"Not quite yet," he said, sliding his hand back between her legs, his finger zeroing in on the cream that dripped from her most feminine place and coated his finger with it, drawing it back up to probe her dark entrance.

"No," she said, panicking at the thought.

Not at the thought that it was wrong, but she wanted desperately to feel some part of him back inside her sheath. There was an emptiness between her legs that Gavan had filled so marvelously. She no longer cared where one of their hard lengths went, alone, or together, just so long as something would thrust in and out of her and provide her with the exquisite release of the powerful orgasm lying just beneath the surface.

Caelan deftly massaged her bottom hole, slipping his finger into her, pushing her toward the edge of a climax before withdrawing his attention.

Elizabeth writhed against Gavan, who held her fast in tortured denial and need.

"Beg me to breach ye with my cock. Beg for yer other husband and I to use you in any way and at any time we choose. Make me believe that ye know your place is between yer two husbands pleasuring them and being pleasured in return."

"Yes, Caelan, please..."

"Say it, Lizzie," rumbled Gavan. "We want to hear ye acknowledge yer place. If ye didna tell us, Cae will continue to play with you for the rest of the night, never quite allowing you to reach that pinnacle of pleasure yer body is demanding. We'll leave ye wet and wanting until ye break down and beg."

Trying to stifle her tears of frustration, she took a ragged breath. "Please, Caelan; please, take me."

"Who do you belong to, Lizzie?" Caelan whispered.

"You and you. Both of you."

"Good girl, Lizzie," intoned Gavan.

"Let's get ye up on your knees, Lizzie. Gavan's going to hold ye while I plow ye from behind."

"No, please, Caelan," she said, suddenly afraid and tucking her tail.

"She thinks ye want her arse," said Gavan.

"Nay, lass, yer not ready for that, but, in time. Tonight, I just want to fuck ye cunny like Gav did, and you liked it when he stroked yer cunny, didn't ye? Let me bring ye the same kind of pleasure."

She nodded, burying her head against Gavan's chest as he held her, stroking her hair and lifting her face to his for a kiss. Elizabeth heard a kind of gravelly purr coming from Caelan as he parted her ass cheeks and stroked downward, stopping to swirl around her back entrance before continuing down to expose her swollen vulva.

"Ye left our bride swollen and covered in yer seed, Gav. Gawd, she's so beautiful. We are the most fortunate of men to have such a fine girl as our bride."

Elizabeth groaned in frustration, prompting both her husbands to chuckle.

Caelan, once more, parted her lower lips and probed her entrance, drawing forth her natural lubricant and coating his cock with it.

"Easy, lass. Let me fill ye and bring ye pleasure," Caelan crooned.

Kneeling behind her, Caelan grasped her hips to hold her in place as he lined up his staff with her sheath and thrust forward, burying himself deep within her. She caught her breath, as her pussy had just so recently been breached for the first time. Elizabeth should have been trying to get away from him. Instead, his dominant possession of her made her scream in ecstasy as her body shuddered with a tremendous orgasm.

He stayed still, allowing her body to begin to recover. Caelan then drew back and surged forward again.

"Good girl, Lizzie. Ye like it when yer husbands fuck ye, don't ye?" he groaned.

"Yes," she cried.

"Tis nothing wrong in that, Lizzie. A wife should be able to enjoy the attention of her husbands and know that her happiness and pleasure is foremost in their thoughts," agreed Gavan.

Caelan's forceful thrusting provided a combination of exquisite joy, tinged with discomfort. She arched her back in primal response to his claiming as he surged forward again. Each time as the tip of his cock hit her cervix, she could feel his cock swelling even larger.

He was in complete and utter control, her body merely the receptacle for his lust and pleasure. Caelan continued to plow her pussy with his mighty staff; his control seemed to be eroding. He grasped her hips harder and drove into her, repeatedly slamming into her. Elizabeth's body was rocked by the power of her response to him. She was unprepared for her body's ability to recover, only to begin the process of climaxing again.

Elizabeth clung to Gavan, who continued to hold and kiss her. One hand stole underneath her, and he played with her nipples, pinching and tugging as they'd discovered she liked. He had figured it out without her having to verbalize it. She was past thought, beyond the ability to form words, but she knew, in her soul, she'd been meant for this. Caught between two men, used by them, pleasured by them.

She moaned as Caelan continued to drive into her, causing her to orgasm repeatedly. It didn't take long for Elizabeth to lose herself to the physical sensations he continued to elicit from her and to lose count of how many times she climaxed. Combined with the cock being used to toss her into the whirlwind of an orgasmic storm was the one beneath her becoming engorged again.

At last, Caelan's cock seemed to have doubled in size inside of her. He rammed into her, sinking his shaft as deep as he could get it and waited for a moment.

The sensation bordered on painful, until she felt his cum spurting into her, coating and bathing the ravaged walls of her pussy. Caelan had ceased moving his hips, but she could feel his cock pumping his seed deep into her body. Her sheath began to pulse in time to his release so that it, too, worked to catch his semen as deeply within her as it could.

When at last he had finished, he kissed the nape of her neck.

At the same time, Gavan kissed her mouth.

Caelan uncoupled from her gently, lying down on one side of the big bedroll.

Gavan lifted her off his body and placed her between them as he laid down on her other side.

Exhaustion and physical exertion claimed her as her husbands settled down on either side, snuggling against her. She knew she would be sore, but she had never felt as sated and content in her life. For the first time in her life, she knew she belonged.

4

CAELAN

THE NEXT MORNING, Caelan sat by the campfire, setting the coffee on to perk and setting out the things they would have for breakfast. Gavan had walked down to the creek to wash off the night's excesses. Caelan glanced over at their beautiful bride, twirling his wedding band around his finger.

"Gawd, there's a part of me that wishes like hell she hadn't been a virgin last night," said Gavan as he rejoined him.

"Can I guess which part?" Caelan quipped.

"Aye, the same part of yers that wishes the same thing. She was spectacular, wasn't she?"

"She was, indeed," agreed Caelan. "I didna think anything has ever felt as good as sinking my shaft in her cunt. Ye shattered her maidenhead. She was slick with yer seed, and ye stretched her good. But, still, her cunny fit my cock like a custom-made glove. I want to get her home and start training her arse. I want to fuck her there while ye take her pussy."

Gavan nodded. "Aye. Did ye bring any of the plugs? It probably wouldn't hurt her if she wore a small one for a bit this morning."

"We are planning to stay for a few days, are we not?"

"I think she needs to rest. She was exhausted last night, and not just from our claiming. But I know ye are keen to claim her arse, and it wouldna hurt her to start getting used to the idea not only that her body belongs to us now, but that she will mind. I didna think she's had a lot of that in her life."

"I agree. Poor lass was just left with no one to help or guide her. I did bring the two smallest plugs, not knowing what ye had planned. I don't think taking a few days here would hurt anything. I cabled Bridgewater and told them we were claiming our bride and might well be a few days getting home. Besides, she canna have slept well being in jail like that," said Caelan.

"We may have used her hard last night, but I'll nae say she didn't sleep well after. Did ye see how she curled between us like she'd always been there?"

Caelan smiled. "Ye do know the chances of her waking up and being the sweet, compliant girl we ended up snuggled next to last night are slim to none."

Gavan chuckled. "I wouldna place any money on slim. I suspect the spitting wildcat will be back, in spades. She's most likely to be embarrassed by her reaction, and a wee bit sore. Neither of us would be considered small."

"Aye, but I do think we should get credit for not having her repeatedly last night."

"I agree. I think I'm harder for her now than I was last night, when I saw her lying back against you; her nipples stiff, skin flushed, and pussy on display..." He ended the sentence with a sigh.

"Speaking of which, do ye think we should shave her lady bits? I like running my fingers through those silky curls but, bare, her beauty can't be hidden from us."

Nodding, Gavan answered, "I agree. We can give that some thought. If we decide we want her bare, we could do it when we plug her arse. I'll do the shaving, and ye can start training her sweet arse."

"I may well spend some time later introducing her to sucking cock. I'm like you; now that I've had her, I canna wait to have her again. As we've all the privacy in the world, we may as well keep the lass naked."

"Aye, that way, at least, we can enjoy her beauty."

———

ELIZABETH

ELIZABETH'S EYES FLUTTERED OPEN. She couldn't believe the sun was up, not rising, but having already cleared the horizon. It took her a moment to remember she wasn't in a jail cell and not scheduled to hang. When she remembered why she wasn't going to die, and the two men with whom she had shared the momentous night before, and what they had done, she felt herself blush from the tips of her toes to the roots of her hair. She sniffed and smelled coffee.

Gavan knelt down beside her, with Caelan taking up a position on the other side. Gavan lifted her body up gently and slid beneath and behind her, cradling her in his arms like she was the most precious thing in the world.

"Here, sweetheart, I brought ye some coffee. There's nae cream for it, but I do have sugar, molasses, or chocolate, if ye'd like," said Caelan, offering her a mug.

"Chocolate?" she asked.

She'd only had that sweet treat a few times but, each time, she had savored it.

"Aye," he grinned. "Gavan has a serious addiction to the stuff. Instead of cream, or sugar, he adds a couple of dollops of chocolate."

"Try it," Caelan urged. "I'll bet you like it. Let it sit in the mug for a moment or two to melt and, then, swirl it around to mix it in."

Caelan handed her the mug and then fished out a small container which had the confection in it.

Elizabeth did as he told her before taking a small sip. It was heavenly. There was a slight breeze, and as it passed over her bare skin, Elizabeth realized she was still naked. The things they had done, things they had said all came rushing back to her, and she threw the coffee at Caelan and tried to escape from Gavan's embrace.

Instead of being angry, or upset, both men laughed, as Gavan tightened his arms around her, keeping her in place. She could feel his hard cock pressing against the front of his trousers, and realized Caelan was in the same state.

"Let go of me," she snarled.

"Nae, Lizzie. And that's no way to act, or speak, to either of us."

"No," she wailed, ineffectively trying to pry his hands from around her.

"Do ye think her nipples are pebbled because of the breeze, or just wanting some attention?" Caelan asked with a grin plastered across his face.

Elizabeth managed to throw an elbow into Gavan's chest, causing him to exhale sharply.

"Lizzie! That's enough. You can either settle down, sit in my lap, and have some breakfast, or I'll put you over my knee and spank your pretty bottom. And it is a pretty bottom, isn't it, Cae?"

"Aye. 'Tis beautiful, especially when viewed from behind when yer giving her a good plowing. It'll be even better when it isn't her cunny I'm taking." Caelan reached out and traced her areola with his fingertip.

Elizabeth squirmed, kicked, and batted at Caelan's hand, desperate to get away from them both.

"Lizzie, I told you to behave," said Gavan with a tone that, while calm, had iron running beneath it.

"I want my clothes. He can't just touch me whenever he wants."

Caelan crouched down so he was eye level with her. "Aye, lass, I can. Yer my wife, and I will touch ye whenever, wherever, and however I choose, as will Gavan."

Elizabeth balled her fist and lunged as far forward as

Gavan's strong arms would allow. Had Caelan not rocked back on his heels, she may well have broken his nose. She thought, for a moment, she had broken free of Gavan, when she was summarily spun around and tossed over his lap, face down.

Before she could form the requisite words, or any kind of defense, he brought his hand crashing down on her exposed rump. With one hand, he held her upper body down over his hard thighs and, with the other, he collided with her still tender backside.

Gavan began to spank her as he had in the jail cell only, this time, she was naked and could feel the fresh air all around her. Elizabeth could not believe he was doing this again. He rhythmically, and steadily, covered her backside with blow after stinging blow. She wasn't able to keep from crying for nearly as long as she had previously, but the worst part was that her arousal had kicked in stronger than before.

His hand landed targeted swats to her behind before it worked its way down to the juncture of her bottom and her legs. He delivered several well aimed smacks to that sensitive spot, which produced a howl in response before he continued down and punished the backs of her thighs as well.

"Gavan, please. I'll behave."

All she wanted was for him to stop before the proof of her need started leaking out onto his leg. She glanced up and realized Caelan was watching with keen interest. She could feel Gavan's erection building beneath her. Elizabeth doubted she was fooling either of her husbands. She was sure they knew what she really wanted was for Gavan to quit spanking her and start fucking her again. Nothing had ever felt righter than the feeling that had come over her when her two husbands had each taken a turn mounting her and claiming her as their own.

"Do ye think ye can behave now?" Caelan asked, his brogue thickening.

"Yes. I'm sorry."

Caelan chuckled. "Not as much as yer about to be. Gav and I talked earlier; as we plan to stay here a few days, there's no reason to not start training your arse to take my cock."

Elizabeth's eyes grew wide. "It will never fit."

She watched Caelan walk over to the saddle bags and pull out a small, smooth, highly polished wooden device shaped like a spade. It had what looked to be a handle that led to a wide base and bulged out and then narrowed to a taper. He held it up to show Gavan before returning to them.

Gavan stroked her back gently. "Aye, lass, it will. And Cae will make sure ye take pleasure in the act, but that's why we need to start training yer bottom hole. Trying to punch either of us, or getting away when one of us has ye in his lap, or just wants you close, is going to get ye punished. Sometimes, it will be just a spanking and, then, a good fucking. Other times, something more will be added."

Caelan nodded. "I had planned to start ye out later today with both arse training and cock sucking but, as ye chose to give rein to your nasty temper, in addition to yer spanking, I'm going to plug your bottom hole."

She squirmed and Gavan landed a series of three harsh swats to her rump. Elizabeth yowled. "I hate you," she cried. "I hate you both."

Caelan chuckled as he reached between her legs. "Those stiff nipples, and the gathering dew between yer legs, says otherwise."

As he had the night before, he scooped out some of the slick that seemed to be in abundance whenever he, or Gavan, reached for her. He brought his fingers to his nose and then licked her honey from them before reaching back to get more.

She tensed as he trailed his finger between her butt cheeks and massaged her bottom hole. Elizabeth tried to move away, but Gavan had her trapped.

"Nay, Lizzie. We will touch ye wherever we choose, and ye need to accept that."

Caelan pressed against her puckered hole, and she clutched at the blankets, moaning as it gave way and allowed his thumb to enter.

"Caelan? Gavan?" she pleaded softly.

"Is he hurting ye, lass?" asked Gavan.

She shook her head. "I just..."

"Will behave yourself," he completed for her as he pressed his thumb deeper.

"Relax, Lizzie," Caelan said, removing his thumb. "I'm not planning to breach ye with my cock today, but ye need to put yourself in the proper frame of mind."

"And what frame is that?" she asked, bordering on tears.

Both men chuckled before Gavan stroked the crack

between her cheeks and then plunged a finger back in her now relaxed and yielding hole.

She gasped at the unexpected invasion. There was some sting associated with it, and a feeling of fullness she had never experienced back there but, if she were being honest, it wasn't painful, nor was it completely unpleasant.

"The frame that reminds ye that ye've two husbands to please and to mind; that these two husbands love ye and have vowed to protect, cherish, and provide for ye. Part of that includes seeing that yer life is full to the brim with affection and loving. Ye'll be stroked and petted. Yer a beautiful woman, Lizzie. Any man would be proud to be married to ye and would have trouble keeping his hands off ye."

"And ye like our having our hands on ye, don't ye?"

Elizabeth nodded, bit her lower lip, and flexed her fingers into the blankets again. She didn't want to be enjoying this, but she was. There was something incredibly arousing about the way both took command and expected her to accept that. If she didn't do so with good grace, they had both made it clear she would find herself on the wrong end of a spanking.

"There's a good lass," he said, removing his finger and returning to rub her tender backside and the small of her back.

Caelan reached back between her thighs, penetrating her wet heat with two fingers.

"Ach, Gav, she's soaked. I think our wife is not so opposed to having her bottom hole breached as she wants us to believe. Ye are not to lie to us, Lizzie. Wives who lie to their husbands get their bottoms spanked, and a mouthful of soap."

She tensed. Even though a spanking seemed to always make her aroused, she didn't like them and didn't want another.

"Easy Lizzie," soothed Gavan. "Cae was only teasing you about how wet you got when he fingered yer arse. There's nothing shameful in enjoying the loving attentions of yer husbands. But he wasn't teasing about lying."

Caelan removed his fingers and began to slather what he had removed from her pussy over the head of the wooden object. Spreading her cheeks apart, he slowly worked the plug between them, pressing it forward against her dark rosebud before it, too, gave way and allowed him to insert it fully.

Elizabeth gave a soft cry of release. She said nothing, but began to softly cry.

"Shh, Lizzie," crooned Gavan. "There's no need for tears. You were a naughty girl, got your bottom spanked and plugged, and that'll be the end of it."

"Take it out, please?" she wailed.

"Does it hurt?" asked Caelan, clearly concerned.

"No, but it's wrong."

"Not if yer husbands tell ye it isn't and, especially, if they tell ye how fetching it looks between your swollen buttocks and how much it pleases them that yer such a brave lass."

"Take it out, please?"

"Later, Lizzie. It stays in until you've learned your lesson. Then, I'll take it out."

Gavan eased her off his lap and laid her down on her belly with her hips propped up by pillows.

———

CAELAN

CAELAN WATCHED as their beautiful wife began to relax.

"I think I could watch her just lying there with a bright red, plugged bottom for the rest of my life and be content," said Gavan.

"Liar," laughed Caelan. "Ye want to fuck her as bad as I do."

"Maybe more."

"Not possible. I checked her when I was gathering her honey. She's still relatively swollen and tender from last night. But," he said, standing, "I think we agreed she should start learning to suck cock. No time like the present."

He walked back over to her. She gazed up at him, if not with love in her eyes, then at least with her eyes glazed over with lust.

Elizabeth started to push up to stand.

Caelan shook his head and pressed down so that she was kneeling in front of him. He unfastened the front placard to his trousers and lifted his fully engorged cock out, levelling it with her mouth.

"Open," he said.

Elizabeth shook her head.

"Aye, Lizzie, or ye'll earn yerself another spanking and then take my cock in yer mouth."

"But it isn't right," she whimpered.

He crouched down, "It is, sweetheart, if yer husbands say it is, and we do. It's a way for ye to ease our need, especially when we're trying to give yer poor cunny time to recover from last night."

She blushed beat red, clearly uncomfortable with her response.

"Nay, Lizzie, there's not to be embarrassed about. Yer a passionate woman with a desire to please yer husbands and to be pleasured in return. There's nothing wrong with that. And ye were pleasured, were ye not?"

She nodded. "Did I...were you...I mean..."

He took her face in his hands, "Ye were beyond compare."

"But neither of you got...I mean, you stayed..."

Caelan laughed and kissed the tip of her nose. "That's not true, we spent ourselves in ye, and our cocks started to relax and then remembered how they got that way, and wanted more. Ye'll find yer husbands have greedy cocks where fucking ye is concerned."

She smiled and blushed but, this time, understanding the compliment and not being embarrassed.

"Now, because we are good, kind, and concerned husbands, and greedy bastards to boot, I want ye to open yer mouth."

Obediently, and he knew that would be a rare occurrence, she complied, and he gently pushed his cock past her lips and teeth to the back of her throat and groaned as he did so. Holding himself still, he let her adjust to having her mouth full of him with the tip tickling the back of her throat. Caelan steadied her head, not allowing her to move it, languidly fucking her mouth.

"Use your tongue and swirl it around my staff. You can suck on it, too."

Caelan kept her head still but allowed her to find her way to pleasuring him with her mouth. Her inexperience was enchanting and was made up for by her enthusiasm. He groaned heavily as his staff began to bob in her mouth.

The movement startled her, and she tried to draw back.

"Nay, lass, ye'll suck my cock until I've sent my seed down yer throat and into yer belly."

Grasping her long, auburn tresses, he held her still and began to use her mouth more forcefully. As the first of his pre-cum dripped onto her tongue, she momentarily balked.

"Nae, Lizzie, ye will swallow Caelan's seed," said Gavan, breathing heavily, as he watched Caelan fucking her mouth rocking his hips and driving toward the back of her throat.

"Relax yer jaw, Lizzie, and breathe through yer nose. That way, ye can take me more deeply."

Caelan began to increase the tempo of his thrusting. He made noises of deep male gratification and arousal as he took her mouth, and she moaned in harmony, signaling not only her acceptance of his cock in her mouth, but her enjoyment. It was music to his ears. He felt his cock swell as it began shooting his load down her throat. Her look of wonder was captivating. When he finished, he slowly withdrew from her mouth.

Without a word spoken, or any gesture given, Elizabeth crawled on all fours until she was directly in front of Gavan, eye level with his straining cock, and then rocked back onto her heels.

"I think ye did a good job teaching our wife to suck cock."

"She's a natural. I think our kitty wants some more cream, don't ye, lass?"

Elizabeth said nothing but reached for the front of Gavan's trousers, which were tented by his swollen member. When he nodded, she used tentative fingers to unbutton the placard and lifted his cock out. She smiled as she felt it felt warm and alive in her hand as it pulsed, the veining in sharp relief to the smooth skin.

"Wrap you hand around the base, Lizzie, and squeeze him gently. Yer men's cocks like to be held firmly, but not too tight. Now, take the head of his staff in yer mouth and suck and lick it the way you did mine."

As she followed Caelan's instructions, Gavan groaned and fisted her hair. She stopped, unsure of herself.

"Nay, lass, yer pleasing him. If he wants ye to stop, he'll tell ye."

Elizabeth sucked Gavan's throbbing dick back into her mouth, and Gavan moaned deeply, the sound ending in a sigh.

"Good, lass," Gavan managed to say as he began to thrust forward, pushing his cock past where she had been comfortable.

When she tried to pull back, Caelan put his hand on

the back of her head, urging her forward, sliding her mouth down the length of his shaft.

Lizzie groaned, and Gavan's cock twitched in response.

"There's a good lass," Caelan purred as he continued to push her head forward, impaling her mouth on Gavan's member.

She was able to take several more inches in her mouth.

Watching her suck Gavan, Caelan was becoming more aroused by the minute. While he had no interest in even touching Gavan's rod, guiding Lizzie's head and gently forcing her to take more of it than she had originally wanted was arousing in the extreme. Her lips and tongue enveloped Gavan's thick, throbbing flesh, and Caelan looked at Gavan, who was as mesmerized by their young bride as he was.

"Harder," Gavan growled, clenching his teeth, closing his eyes, and leaning his head back.

Caelan released his hold and watched Lizzie draw her head back, licking along Gavan's length, lapping her tongue all around the head.

Gavan flexed his fingers in her hair, taking complete control of her movements. He surged forward again and again, faster and faster. Gavan growled again, pumping harder and arching his back to thrust even more deeply. Caelan could tell when Gavan started sending long, ropes of cum down their bride's gullet and into her belly, where it would mix with his own.

When he stilled, and removed his cock from her mouth, Gavan leaned over, pushing the hair out of her eyes and dropping several kisses, one each on the top of her head, the tip of her nose, and finally her lips.

Gavan locked eyes with Caelan, "Aye, Cae, ye taught her very well."

Caelan chuckled and stroked Elizabeth's hair. "Ye go lay back down, Lizzie. I'll make something for breakfast, and the three of us will eat together. Would ye like that?"

Gavan walked over to the bedroll and put himself in the same position Caelan had been last night when Gavan had taken her maidenhead. He crooked his fingers at her to coax her to come to him.

Elizabeth crawled back on his lap and curled up.

5

*E*LIZABETH

ELIZABETH SPENT the next few days enthralled in a sexual haze. She might have been mortified, if not for Gavan and Caelan's constant assurance that nothing that happened between the three of them was wrong. She found she craved their touch and was rarely without one, or the other, touching her.

After the first day, she lost her shyness about being naked in their presence. They had decreed that, while she could wear a corset and chemise in the future, she would be allowed no bloomers. Usually, Caelan had on both trousers and shirt, but Gavan tended to favor just his trousers. He teased her that, if she wasn't careful, he'd take to wearing a kilt, a kind of male skirt he could easily ruck out of the way to have her anytime he liked.

Part of her still fretted that what they were doing was

wrong but, each time they touched her and murmured words of sex and love to her, those feelings slipped further and further away. After letting her recover the first day from the loss of her virginity, they began to regularly fuck her several times during the day and night.

There were times, it would be one-on-one and, other times, both would be there as one fucked her pussy and the other played with her nipples, clit, or bottom hole. Both Gavan and Caelan woke with morning hard ons and both insisted on plowing her pussy, or cunny, as they called it, often not bothering to wake her before they started. Elizabeth decided that was the best way to be awakened.

Gavan usually had her on her back with her thighs spread wide so all three could see his cock disappearing and reappearing into her pussy. Caelan, most often, had her on her knees and mounted her like a wild stallion. They encouraged her to tell them what she liked best. The problem was, she liked it all.

Each morning, when they were through, Gavan would take her over his lap while Caelan used their combined essence to lubricate the plug before placing it inside her. She had to wear it for several hours, and they gently teased her when she squirmed.

"Our Lizzie likes having her bottom plugged, don't ye, lass?" Caelan said one morning as he fisted her hair to drag her over to where Gavan was lying prone. "Suck yer husband's cock, Lizzie."

She had leaned down, deep throating his staff, loving the feel and taste of him. She had discovered that her husbands tasted different. Caelan's cum was sweeter and less salty, but she found she liked both. Her head bobbed up and down, taking him deeper in her mouth while swirling her tongue around it like a lollipop.

Elizabeth was so focused on pleasuring Gavan that she startled when Caelan stroked her back down between her butt cheeks and jiggled the plug.

"Cae," she panted before yowling when he swatted her.

"Nay, lass, ye keep sucking Gavan and pleasuring him."

He twisted the plug inside her, and she found she could barely focus on even keeping Gavan's cock in her mouth, but Gavan grasped her head and forced it down the length of his staff.

Caelan knelt behind her and nudged her thighs apart. " 'Tis time ye learned to pleasure the both of us at the same time and to take pleasure in all three holes at once. Ye have Gavan's cock in yer mouth, the wee plug up your bum, and now you'll take my cock in yer cunny. Do ye want my cock in ye, Lizzie, stroking you so that Gav and I both fill you up at the same time?"

She nodded and mewled in need.

"Keep sucking, Lizzie. Cae will see to yer need, won't ye, Cae?"

"Aye, Gav, I will," he said as he guided his cock into her wet, warm cunny and began stroking rapidly.

Elizabeth felt both of their cocks swelling and twitching in anticipation of their shooting their loads in her.

"Ye didna let even a drop of my seed leave yer mouth,

lass. Take it deep and into yer belly while Cae fills your cunny."

She managed not to choke on his cock as he started spurting his cream down her throat while Caelan began filling her pussy.

When they were finished, she was sprawled across Gavan's prone body.

After supper, they would take turns fucking her, sometimes hard and fast, and sometimes slow and long. Elizabeth didn't care. As long as they fucked her repeatedly, she fell into a stupor because she had been so well used and pleasured. They constantly praised her, and she began to bask in their loving attention.

Each night, she would curl into their collective arms, exhausted and sated. Gavan mostly laid on his back, and she curled against him, with her head on his shoulder. Caelan spooned with her from the back. She had never felt so warm, safe, and loved in her entire life.

If her husbands liked having their hands on her, she was finding just as much pleasure in touching them. She kept waiting to feel as if they were just using her, or were going to withdraw, or abandon her, like every other person in her life, but they never did. In fact, they did just the opposite, they were gentle and loving with her, always ensuring her needs were seen to first.

———

GAVAN

. . .

GAVAN WOKE to find himself all alone with their bride. They were planning to leave today. Caelan had said he wanted to go back into town and get Lizzie a few more things so she'd have more than the one skirt and her tight-fitting chaps to wear, although they agreed they might keep the chaps on hand for her to wear just for them, preferably with nothing else on.

His cock throbbed against the crack of her arse and, in her sleep, she snuggled back against him.

Gavan smiled as he got up on his knees behind her, drawing her hips up so she was in the perfect position to be mounted. He parted her thighs and sank his length into her. He began to stroke her deeply, and her body responded as it always did, orgasamming from his dominant possession. As she woke, he began thrusting harder and faster, quickly bringing her to a second climax before driving into her with an even greater frenzy in order to achieve his own release.

Once he was finished, and the quivering of her pussy ceased, he patted her backside, slid from inside her, nipped her ear, and whispered, "Good morning, wife."

She giggled, a sound he and Caelan agreed she only made when happy and sated.

"Good morning, husband." She sat up. "Where is my other husband?"

"What?" he said in false indignation. "I'm not enough for ye, ye wanton hussy?"

Elizabeth giggled again. "Nay, yer not," she said, mocking his brogue.

"Thank God for that," said Caelan as he rode in and

overheard their banter. Leaping off his horse, he tossed his reins to Gavan.

———

CAELAN

CAELAN STARTED to position Lizzie more to the center of the bed. Uncharacteristically, she pulled away from him.

He and Gavan had counted themselves amongst the most fortunate of men. Lizzie was beautiful, intelligent, capable, and wildly passionate. She reveled in their amorous attention and took to most things willingly. She was still apprehensive about his taking her arse, but the idea of having his cock in her arse while Gavan fucked her cunny seemed to make her inordinately wet. He and Gavan had decided the first time they doubly penetrated her, with neither using her mouth, would be in the big bed they'd had built for their use at Bridgewater.

Lizzie sprang up and spun away from him, dancing away as he reached for her.

He growled but, before the sound had left his mouth, she stepped back onto the bedroll, dropping gracefully onto her knees, arching her back, and moaning before stretching down into position and spreading her legs. God, she was magnificent. Her needy vulva pulsed and, beyond it, her glorious pussy offering a wet, creamy invitation for him to mount and breed.

Caelan accepted without reservation, mounting her

in one swift, strong move, his groin slamming into her backside as he held her tight.

Her response was as primitive as it was powerful; she cried out his name as she orgasmed.

He pistoned his hips so that his cock began to hammer her pussy. He hadn't been this rough with her before, but she surprised him by welcoming it. She cried out as he pumped his hips, which seemed only to inflame her lust.

His hold on her tightened as he thrust more deeply within her. He fucked her through two more climaxes without let up, not even allowing her to catch her breath. The feelings of passion, possession, and dominance were intense. Over and over, he stroked her cunt with a fierce and overwhelming need to not only breed her, but reclaim her, as well. Locking her to him, he pumped his seed deep into her.

As he withdrew, he realized Gavan was standing behind them, raw lust evident in every fiber of his being.

"Ye should be careful how ye tease Gavan, lass. I fear yer nay getting off your knees until he's had ye again."

Lizzie looked at the man who was both partner and brother to Caelan and, with a sensual smile that was as old as time, she purred, "Then, you'd best get out of his way so he can fuck me."

Caelan stood, slapping her ass with a bit of sting then hitched up his pants.

Gavan practically threw him aside as he dropped behind Lizzie, opened his trousers, and rammed home with his cock.

Lizzie squealed in aroused delight before succumbing to her orgasm and screaming his name.

Caelan got great pleasure watching Gavan have at Lizzie. Never before had the son of the Laird of the Clan MacLean given into his baser side, or allowed his heart to become engaged. Caelan hid his smile. There was no doubt in his mind that, at long last, Gavan had fallen in love.

When he was finished, Gavan had encouraged Lizzie to stretch out. As she did, he stroked her body like one would a cat, and their bride purred in pleasure.

Calen joined them, lying down next to her.

"I went back into town and picked ye up a few things," said Caelan.

"I don't want anything from that fucking shithole of a town," she spat.

Gavan's hand descended on her upturned rump with the speed of a striking rattler.

She rolled over, spoiling for a fight. "God damn it, Gavan!" she snarled.

Without a word, Gavan stood up, pulled on his trousers and boots and then hauled Lizzie up by her hair, striding for the creek where they had left soap and cloths for her to be able to take a bath later. She had requested one the day before.

"Caelan?" she asked quietly.

"Aye, lass," he said kissing her forehead before dipping his head and taking her nipple into his mouth.

"You and Gavan have had a bath, and Gavan said there's a big tub at home, but could I go wash up in the creek?"

"Maybe in the morning."

"But why..."

"Didna fuss at me, Lizzie," he said in a low growl.

"I'm not clean... I have..." she stumbled over what to say.

"Ye have some of our spend in your short curls."

"After this morning, it's not the only place, and it's itchy."

Caelan had grinned. "Aye, ye remember that the next time you think to get uppity."

Lizzie stomped her foot, and Caelan had swatted her ass. Gavan was right, their Lizzie had a fine ass for spanking and, as soon as he got her home, he meant to enjoy her arse for fucking. They'd come to know their Lizzie loved having them pump their seed in her. She got the most rapturous, glazed-over look when they spilled themselves in her. She would sigh like the proverbial alley cat.

Earlier in the day, her defiant streak had reared its ugly head over a simple request he made of her. When she wouldn't back down, they spit roasted her between them. Gavan had fucked her mouth, and Caelan had given her cunny a good ramming.

When he was ready to release himself, Caelan had pulled out and sprayed her back with his essence.

Gavan did the same, except hauled her up on her knees and covered her glorious titties. Even though they'd brought her to climax, she'd thrown a veritable tantrum. Gavan had grasped her about the waist, bending her over his hip, and Caelan spanked her pretty bottom to a bright red. Once her temper dissolved into remorse with tears and promises to behave, he let up.

They both folded her into their embrace, and she'd sobbed, truly sorry for her outburst.

"There now, lass. Ye know better and, now, you know

what happens to wives who get too big for their britches," Gavan consoled her as Caelan collected the butt plug. When he bent her over his knee, and Caelan had parted her cheeks, she knew what was coming. She didn't protest at all as he'd slid the larger of the two plugs into her pussy, twisting it to coat it well with her juices, and then seated it in her bottom hole.

"Now, ye go get on the bedroll, and ye think about having that plug up yer arse and that misbehaving and throwing tantrums have consequences."

Lizzie tromped over to the bedroll, started to sit, thought better of it, considering the state of her backside, and glared at both, clearly pouting. They stood side by side.

"I didna think the lass has taken the lesson of the thrashing to heart," Gavan said.

"Nay, but there's more than one way to humble our wife. Wife," he called, "Ye stretch out on yer belly and spread yer legs. Show yer husbands what a sweet cunny and arse you have for their use."

He watched her struggle to contain her temper. Once she had it under control, she did as he told her. They left the plug in until after supper, making her help with cooking and chores without relief. She went from upset to sore to desperate for relief all right before their eyes.

In the end, Gavan had sat on the log and made Lizzie impale herself on his cock, sitting in his lap. Caelan removed the plug and then fingered her arse while Gavan moved her up and down his length.

She climaxed and howled repeatedly, calling their names.

When Gavan finished, he lifted her off his cock, tossed her over his knee, and held her while Caelan had fucked her mouth shooting a torrent of cum into her belly.

Now here they were the next day, confronted by her bad temper, again. Gavan had Lizzie by the roots of her hair as he strode toward the creek. Caelan imagined there'd be washing, but it would be her mouth and not her body.

Realizing his intent, Lizzie struggled and tried to dig her feet in.

Gavan simply transferred her mane from one hand to the other and spanked her the rest of the way to the creek.

Caelan followed and tried not to laugh.

Lizzie had become quite contrite and was trying to get Gavan not to soap her mouth. She failed miserably.

"How many times have I told ye, yer not to use that kind of language?" When Lizzie said nothing, Gavan had swatted her backside several times, making her howl and hiccup soap bubbles. "Have ye not been told repeatedly?"

"Yes, Gavan. I'm sorry, but I hate that town."

"And that's fine and good to say, but ye didna need to use foul language."

He'd marched her over to Caelan, handing her off.

"Yer the one that rode into town to get her something nice. It's time she learned I'm not the only one who'll take her over his knee when she's in need of correction."

Caelan had nodded, taken Lizzie by the hand, and nodded. "Aye," was all he said before heading to the uprooted tree, which made a natural bench for sitting, fucking, or spanking. Lizzie had already sat and been fucked leaning over it. It was only natural that one of them would need to use it to pull her over his knee and spank her bottom.

"Caelan, please, no. I'm sorry I cursed."

"Aye. I imagine ye'll be a lot sorrier before I'm through."

———

ELIZABETH

CAELAN PULLED her over his knee and began to spank her. If she'd thought the swats Gavan had given her thus far were painful, the spanking Caelan was inflicting demonstrated a new level of pain.

Elizabeth kicked and screamed and tried everything she could think of to get away from him. She wriggled and squirmed and did her best to get free. But hard as she tried, she could not escape Caelan's presence, or his hand that continued to punish her backside.

Caelan focused on the fleshiest part of her cheeks and only placed a few swats to her delicate sit spots.

She endured blow after blow. She screamed and wailed, but managed to keep from cursing and, still, the spanking continued. All the while, he spoke soothingly to her. He reminded her that she was being spanked because she'd been naughty but, when it was over, she would be fucked, and all would be forgiven.

Finally, she quit fighting him and went limp over his knee. It still hurt, and she could feel every swat. The moment she capitulated and let the tears fall, Caelan stopped.

"Ye want her over the tree, or across my knee?" Caelan asked Gavan.

"She's fine where she is," was his response.

Elizabeth grimaced when Gavan got behind her, parted her legs, and rubbed her bottom. Then, with his cock poised at her entrance, he grasped her hips and surged forward.

She cried out as his pelvis hit her punished backside and she grabbed Caelan's leg to not feel as though she would fall as Gavan plunged into her fast and hard, only allowing her a single climax before he drove deep and began pumping his seed into her.

Gavan withdrew and he gave her a hard swat between her legs. "If there's a next time, Lizzie, ye'll get a taste of leather across yer behind. Ye ken?"

She nodded and waited, knowing she had yet to mollify Caelan. He removed her from his lap.

"Put yer hands on the log, Lizzie, spread yer legs, and present yer pussy to me."

"Caelan," she mewled.

"Have ye not been spanked hard enough?"

"No," she wailed and then put herself in position.

Caelan wasted no time in coming up behind her, kicking her legs apart to make room. He parted her thighs and opened the front of his trousers. His cock sprang out, and he sank into her wet heat, groaning in ecstasy.

She called for him again but this time in surrendered abandon and not in distress.

"There's my good girl," he crooned as he began to thrust in and out of her, riding her through several orgasms before his cock began to swell and twitch. "One more, Lizzie, come for yer husband while he fucks ye."

Her explosive orgasm triggered his, and he butted her punished ass several times as he spurted his seed into her. Caelan straightened as he spilled the last of himself into her.

When he was finished, he uncoupled from her.

Knowing better than to get up, she reached her hand back, wanting and needing his reassurance.

He took her hand in his.

"I'm sorry, Caelan. That's a long ride, and you were trying to do something nice."

"Aye, lass, I was," he said as he released her hand and headed toward their cookfire.

She started to cry.

Caelan returned to her and drew her up off the log.

Elizabeth collapsed into him and wound her arms around him, trying to get as close as possible. She reached behind her, reaching for Gavan in an attempt to draw him in.

He hesitated and then relented, wrapping himself around her as well.

"Ye didna please either of yer husbands with that display of temper," growled Gavan.

"I know, I'm sorry. They wanted to kill me," she said, petulantly.

Both of her husbands chuckled. "You stole their cattle, their horses, and their money," they said in unison.

She peeked up at Caelan, and then over her shoulder at Gavan. "But, other than that, what did they have against me?" she asked in her most innocent tone, batting her big green eyes at them.

Both men laughed.

"Caelan, can I please go take a bath?"

"Did ye ask Gav?"

"Well, yes," she started, but was cut off when Caelan swatted her.

"Ye didna play us against one another. If ye asked Gav and he said no, then it is Gav who must rescind his denial."

"I'm sorry, Gav. I wasn't trying to do that. I wasn't thinking."

"Forgiven, lass. And, yes, ye may go and take a bath, but do not tarry, and do not wander far. Ye stay within earshot. Do not venture much beyond the bend. There's a good spot with a rock where you can sit to bathe."

"But it's deeper farther upstream, and I can swim."

"The current is too swift, Lizzie. Ye didna ask for permission to go swimming. Ye asked to take a bath. Yer not to venture upstream. Ye have not had yer bottom spanked when its wet and fresh from a bath. I can tell ye, the water will intensify the effect. Keep that in mind, Lizzie."

She headed down to the creek and found the place Gavan had indicated. It was shallow and, not only couldn't she swim, it wasn't even deep enough to submerge herself to rinse.

She continued on upstream until she found an ideal place. It had easy passage into the water and was deep enough to rinse and play in the water. It was bracingly cold, but the towels and washcloth Caelan had purchased in town for her were soft, like velvet.

Elizabeth dove into the water and swam for a few moments, allowing the water and its swift-moving current to rush over her skin, refreshing and cleaning it. She was completely wet and stood close to shore where the water trickled over the pebbles in the sand, leaning over to wash her hair and using the cloth to clean herself.

She smiled as she considered her life. She had two men who said they loved her, and she believed them. She had a new home that sounded beautiful. Gavan had described a huge tub that would hold all of them. Elizabeth blushed when she recalled his description of the wickedly erotic things they would do to and with her in the hot water. Her beaded nipples ached for their attention. She was just rinsing off when she heard the sound of someone else entering the water. Elizabeth turned, expecting to see one, or both, of her husbands.

Nude and having just rinsed out her hair, she turned smiling, "Ready for more?"

Instead, she was confronted by Sheriff Gutherie.

"You have no idea, bitch," he said swinging the butt-end of his rifle into her jaw, knocking her senseless.

6

 AVAN

"Cae, shouldn't Lizzie be back from her bath? I could understand a delay if we were at home and she was soaking in that huge tub ye insisted we buy. But that creek water is cold."

"Ach, yer just feeling randy and want another go at our girl," he laughed.

"Always," Gavan agreed with a smile. "But she should have been back by now. Ye didna think she's gone further than I told her she could go?"

"Maybe. She's still testing us to see if we'll make her mind."

"Ye think that's all it is? Ye didna think she wants to leave us, do ye?"

His friend crossed to him. "Nay, Gav. I knew she hasn't

said it, but Lizzie loves us, and she loves her life with us. We dote on her. Yer far more indulgent with her than I would have thought."

"She's had a hard life, Cae. Everyone always telling her what she couldn't be and ripping her away from people she cared about. She had to become hard in order to survive. Everyone in her life has abandoned or disappointed her. We need to give her some time to see we're different and she has no need to keep us at bay for we'll never hurt her."

Caelan shook his head. "I don't agree. It made her strong and gave her a brittle shell, but there are cracks in it already. She reaches for one or both of us when she has a bad dream. She likes to snuggle between us at night and is so responsive when either of us reaches for her. And the look she gets on her face when one of us fills her with our seed. 'Tis a wonder to behold."

Gavan smiled. "Aye, the lass does like to fuck. She's a veritable alley cat in heat..."

Caelan chucked. "And we're the tom cats looking to make her howl as we breed her."

"Did ye ever think we'd find a lass as fine as she?"

"Not in my wildest dreams."

"I think I'll go make sure she's all right," said Gavan.

He left Caelan and made his way down to the creek, expecting to find her just around the bend. Gavan swore when she wasn't there and followed her footprints upstream until he found a place that had an easy entrance into the fast running water and was deep enough for Lizzie to go swimming. He had to admit it was a better bathing spot than the one he'd told her to use, but he'd need to punish her for disobeying.

"Lizzie, where are ye?"

He looked around and could see no sign of her still there. He called for her again; only the sound of the rushing water responded. Lizzie was nowhere to be found. Had she run from them? Had the past few days been her simply lulling them into a sense of false security so they'd let their guard down and she could escape? Gavan made a preliminary search of the area and then ran back to the camp.

"Caelan, she's gone."

"What do ye mean gone?"

"She's not there, not at the creek. She played us. She used us to escape the hangman, then lulled us into believing that she wanted to be with us. She played us false."

"Gav, yer making a lot of assumptions, and none of them in her favor. I didna believe Lizzie capable of what yer accusing her of. Despite the outlaw face she showed to the world, she's a sweet thing, and I think already has feelings for us, both of us. She has a wildly passionate, naughty steak, but there isn't a mean, nor truly deceitful, bone in her body."

"She's a rustler and a thief," Gavan countered, angrily. "We never should have trusted her. Just kept her confined to our bed where we could fuck her and sire children on her. Saddle up yer horse and let's get after her. When we catch up with her, I'm going to take my belt to her backside and lay a set of stripes on it she won't forget any time soon." With a great deal of agitation, he began to saddle his horse. Muttering his breath, he continued, "After that, I'm going to fuck her until she can't walk, much less run away."

Without a word, Caelan walked over to his partner of many years, turned him away from his horse and toward him, and punched him in the mouth, knocking him onto the ground.

"What the fuck, Caelan!" Gavan said springing back to his feet with balled fists.

"Ye didna talk about our bride that way. Lizzie has done nothing since ye wed her to warrant that kind of distrust from ye. If Lizzie is missing, and that's still questionable, what makes ye think something hasn't happened to her? What makes ye think that she's played ye false? For Christ's sake, she's naked and has no clothes! Have ye done something that would make her run? The lass has exceeded every fantasy either of us ever had about a shared wife and seemed to be well on her way to giving us her heart and soul. And, at the first sign of trouble, ye make accusations and threats? What the fuck is wrong with ye?"

Gavan felt the blow from Caelan's words far more harshly than he had the fist in his face. He looked at his oldest and best friend and felt ashamed. Caelan was right, Lizzie had done nothing to deserve his mistrust.

Holding up his hands, he said, "Yer right, Cae. The lass has done nothing wrong that I know of and deserves better from her husband than to be accused until we know the truth of it. I just...she wasn't there..."

"And yer madly in love with her and terrified that,

since we forced her into this arrangement, she's going to leave."

Gavan nodded. "Aye. I tried telling myself that it was just my cock she had from the get-go, but it isn't true. I love her."

"Me, too. Then, let's go find her. Let's see what happened and, whatever it is, we'll figure out a way to make it right for her, even if that means we lose her."

"Aye. I'll apologize to her, tell her I love her, and beg her forgiveness, in the hope that she'll stay, but I will accept her decision. And it must be her decision."

The truth of it hung in the air between them. Both men saddled their horses and rode back to the place Lizzie had bathed.

———

ELIZABETH

SHE WOKE FEELING GROGGY, not in the sated, happy, and hungover from sex and love groggy, but hit over the head groggy. She was bound and gagged, draped across the front of a horse and wrapped in a scratchy blanket. At least, her husbands had made their bridal bed with soft blankets, silken sheets, and pillows. She smiled, some girls might have wanted a swanky hotel room, but not Lizzie. Her smile widened as she realized she had become their Lizzie and wanted to be no other.

"You're a filthy outlaw and a wanton temptress to boot, living with your gang of thieves and rustlers and now taking up as a fuck toy to two foreigners," Gutherie spat. "Did you like it when they plowed your cunt? Did they do you together, a dick in each hole? You should have hanged, Morgan. I was going to get you to plead for your life and do whatever I told you," he said with a nasty laugh, "and then watched you swing. I'd have fucked your cunt, your ass, and your mouth, and sent you to the gallows dripping my cum. I suppose I could hang you, anyway, when I'm done and blame it on them two pricks, but shooting you is probably safer." He chuckled, "Well, safer for me. Either way, you end up dead, but only after I get to have a go at you."

As abrasive as the blanket was, she was glad of the protection it offered her, at least for the moment. She had to hope that Gavan and Caelan would realize she was missing and come find her. They had saved her from the hangman; she had to pray they'd be in time to save her from the sheriff.

Lizzie wasn't sure how long they rode for; it seemed like hours over rough terrain. Finally, the sheriff rode up a steep incline and into a cavern. In some ways, it was nicer, as it was considerably cooler, but she would have preferred the heat. Out in the open, it would be easier for Gavan and Caelan to find her. She also knew, from her outlaw days, the sheriff was in a far easier position to defend inside the cave.

The sheriff stopped the horse and dismounted. He grabbed the rope that was around her waist and gave it a tug, tossing her on the ground, and knocking the wind out of her.

Lizzie tried to get to her feet.

The sheriff spotted her and kicked her in the back of the knees, throwing her down and forward. He moved away and went to tie his horse to a clump of bushes outside the cavern.

"Stay down, bitch. I gotta hand it to them two foreigners, they know how to treat a woman like you. Keep her naked, spank her ass, and fuck her often. I saw you all this morning. I just don't like to share a woman, but watching this morning while I jerked off was kind of fun. But it just left me wanting to fuck you even more than before. So, when you went off to clean their spunk off you, I came to get you. Them two boys were hung though. Have they fucked your ass yet? I'll bet you didn't like that. Most women don't. But, when you're fucking a whore, it's safer and a tighter fit."

Lizzie said nothing and lay perfectly still. She was terrified on many levels, primarily for her life, and those of Gavan and Caelan. She knew, if the sheriff hurt her, her husbands would kill him. Nothing would stop them. She also feared that, somehow, he would make her recoil from their touch. They loved fucking her, and she enjoyed being fucked by them. Sometimes, it was full of fun and laughter; others it was slow and sensual and full of love; and still others, it was raw and primal. She enjoyed it all and reveled in their care.

The sheriff returned and hauled her to her feet. He untied the restraints and removed the blanket, leaving her naked to his gaze. As comfortable as she had become being in that state of undress with her husbands, having the sheriff stare at her with equal measures of lust and hatred was terrifying.

She moved her hands to try and cover herself from him.

The sheriff knocked her hands away and pinched her nipples, which were tight from the cold.

"Let me get a good look at you. I can see why they wanted you. You're built like a good broodmare; big tits, big hips, and a great ass."

Lizzie looked down and saw the sheriff did not appear to be as aroused as he'd need to be to rape her. He continued fondling her breasts with one hand while he opened the front of his trousers with the other, getting his cock out.

"Did they teach you to suck cock?"

Not trusting her voice, she smiled and nodded.

"I'll bet they did. Get on your knees and get me good and hard. I've been waiting since we caught you for this. If I hadn't had that damn posse with me, I could have saved the town the time and expense of trying you. Hell, if my damn wife's brother hadn't been with us, I probably could have talked the rest of the boys into having a little fun with you before killing you."

Lizzie sat back on her heels. She needed to figure out how to stall for time. The longer this took, the longer she gave Caelan and Gavan to find her. She suppressed a smile; they'd never let her out of their sight again, and she didn't think she'd ever want to be without one of them in reach. She vowed to herself to do whatever she needed to do to stay alive until her husbands could get to her. The sheriff was a dead man, he just didn't know it yet.

"If you're going to kill me, why should I do anything

that will get you hard so you can rape me?" she asked in a quiet voice.

The sheriff backhanded her.

"Because, as long as I'm enjoying myself, you get to live. Now, get back on your knees, slut, and suck my dick," he said as he seated himself on a large rock.

Taking a deep breath and trying to clear her mind, Lizzie lifted the sheriff's limp member from his pants. The smell of stale sweat and urine clung to him. She was a bit surprised at the size of the sheriff's member. She'd known both Caelan and Gavan were well endowed, but the sheriff was downright dinky. Lizzie took a deep breath and wrapped her hand around the base of his cock.

"With your mouth; I can use my own hand."

Deciding that opting for a meek and subservient attitude would serve her best, she dropped her eyes and said, "When Caelan taught me, he had me use my hands and mouth so that he had a nice firm pressure all up and down his shaft. When he wants to come, he has me focus my mouth on the head and then shoves it to the back of my throat to shoot his load down into my belly. He seemed to enjoy it that way."

"Huh, sounds like he taught you pretty good."

"Look, sheriff, we both know I want to stay alive. After all, I agreed to marry two men to keep from being hanged," she said, gently stroking his staff and running her fingers around his balls, which seemed small and shriveled compared to Caelan and Gavan.

"You and I both know that's wrong. You sound like a man with a certain kind of sexual interests that your wife might not appreciate and, being the good man that you are, you don't force it on her. But you're right, I've sinned, and I should be punished, maybe you could help me with that. I wouldn't do anymore stealing, or rustling, no one would know where I was, and I would be available to you whenever you wanted."

She reminded herself her life depended on making the odious man believe she wanted him and would serve him in whatever way he wanted. She vowed she would do whatever it took to stay alive, whatever it took to get back to Caelan and Gavan.

The pink tip of her tongue licked along the underside of the sheriff's member. It stirred under her attention. Lizzie took the head of him into her mouth and swirled her tongue as she sucked, gratified when it began to straighten.

"Damn, girl."

She gave him her best siren's smile as she engulfed half of his length into her mouth, repressing the reflex to gag. It wasn't his size—Gavan and Caelan were both much larger—it was the malodorous stench that emanated from his person. She grasped the remainder in her hand and used both, in concert, to pleasure him.

The sheriff closed his eyes and groaned.

Lizzie closed her eyes and tried to imagine it was one of her husbands. She moved her mouth up and down his length repeatedly; his dick continued to harden.

The sheriff reached out and stroked her hair as he looked at her, his eyes glazed over with lust.

"You are a jezebel, but it might be worth keeping you around," he grunted as began to move his hips in rhythm to her sucking and licking.

Lizzie could feel his rod beginning to thicken and twitch.

"Whore," he said grasping the back of her head to force it further down his length.

"You bastard!" Lizzie heard from behind her.

A bright red hole, dead set between the sheriff's eyes appeared as he fell to the side, his dick slipping past her lips and from her grip. The last part of the expletive was drowned out by the sound of a small derringer being fired.

Lizzie spun around to see the sheriff's pious wife holding a smoking gun, a frozen look on her face. Trying to move out of the line of fire, Lizzie crawled away from the sheriff.

"Is he dead?" the woman asked in an oddly calm tone.

"Yes ma'am," Lizzie said, quietly. "I didn't…"

"Of course, you didn't, child," she said kindly. "Do you have any clothes you can put on?"

"No ma'am. The sheriff took me when I was bathing. My husband," she was able to stop the term from being plural, "and I thought the valley was safe from prying eyes."

The sheriff's wife laughed nervously. "Few could hide from his prying eyes, and he often paid to watch. Let's see if we can't get you clothed."

She walked outside the cave and stopped, backing in slowly.

"Lizzie?" she heard Caelan.

"Cae!" she cried as he rushed past the sheriff's wife and enfolded herself in his arms.

She clung to him, sobbing, all the fear and disgust draining out of her as her tears fell on his broad chest.

"Shh, Lizzie; Gavan and I are here. Can ye stop crying long enough to tell me what happened, and if yer all right?"

She nodded. "He grabbed me at the creek... I should have stayed where Gavan said. The sheriff tied me up... made me...no, I got on my knees..."

Gavan joined them, the sheriff's widow in tow.

He wrapped his arm around her. "Ye did what ye had to do, Lizzie. Ye stayed alive. I'm so proud of ye."

"Aye, yer a brave lass. I didna know many who could have kept their wits around them and done that. I have the things I bought in town, just until we can get something else," said Caelan.

"No, Cae, I was such a bitch this morning. I'm so sorry. It doesn't matter where it came from, it matters that you got it for me."

Caelan left them for a few moments and brought Lizzie something to change into.

Once Lizzie was dressed, Gavan handed the sheriff's widow to Caelan and wrapped the sheriff's body in tattered blanket he'd used to kidnap her.

"So what are we going to do with ye?" Caelan asked the widow.

"I murdered my husband. I'll have to pay for my crime." She reached out and squeezed Lizzie's arm. "I am so sorry for what you had to do. He was a deviant monster. I should have killed him long ago."

"From where we stand, Mrs. Gutherie..."

"Sally, please."

"Sally," Gavan corrected, "Ye saved our Lizzie, and that cancels anything ye did before, and puts us in your debt."

"So, the rumors about Bridgewater are true? Each wife has more than one husband?"

"Yes, I am proud to call both Caelan and Gavan my husbands. No woman was ever so lucky as to have two men as good and honorable as them to love and care for her."

Sally Gutherie shook her head. "I cannot even imagine. I was married to that bastard for almost twenty years. I could never have said that he loved, or cared for me, much less both. And certainly, neither good, nor honorable. You're right Mrs...oh, dear, what do I call you?"

"Eliz..." started Caelan.

"Lizzie," she interrupted him with a grin. "I'm called Lizzie now."

Sally Gutherie smiled. "Lizzie, then. I suppose one of your husbands had best take me back. We can keep your name out of it to avoid the scandal."

"He planned to rape her. There is no scandal to attach to Lizzie. In fact, like Gav said, ye saved her life. Ye've family in town, do ye not?"

"I do..."

"Then, ye go back into town and leave the rest to us. Yer husband had plenty of enemies. We'll make it look like he was ambushed. If burying him is important to ye—"

"His corpse can rot and feed the vultures for all I care," Sally said, vehemently.

"In that case, we'll stage the body where it'll be found, and that'll be the end of it. Ye go on back to town and make sure people see ye. We'll have each other as alibis."

"But won't they be able to tell it was a small gun from the hole in his head?" Sally asked, her eyes shifting around the cavern as if she was afraid someone would overhear.

"We can fix that, Sally. We'll just make it look like a larger gun was used. How long will it take you to get home and be baking bread, or something?"

"A few hours..."

"Then, we'll set up the scene and let it take its own natural course. Ye didna worry yerself. Caelan and I will take care of it."

"I can help," offered Lizzie.

"Nay, lass, ye'll stay out of it and will be with one of us at all times."

"I think I should tell them I shot him and not involve any of you," said Sally.

"There's no need to risk it. And, if ye tell them the whole truth, as ye say, they might try to blame Lizzie. Nay, Sally, yer late husband was a bastard of the first order and deserved to die. Ye did the world a favor, and as Gav said, ye saved Lizzie. We are beholden to ye and will make this right for ye."

"You're sure?" she asked.

"My husbands don't lie. I'll never forget what you did for me, ever. I'm just sorry you had to live with him."

Lizzie took Sally's hand and walked her out to her horse.

Sally mounted and then looked down at her. "When I

first heard about Bridgewater, I thought how awful it must be to have to marry two men and provide them with sexual congress, but you seem not to mind. Is it because they saved you from the noose?" Sally closed her eyes and shook her head. "I'm so sorry. That was incredibly thoughtless and inappropriate of me."

Lizzie grinned. "I wasn't too happy about it at first either but now, even after so short a time, it just seems normal. Gavan is the stern one, and I know, if I misbehave, he will correct me. Caelan is gentler but, if he has to spank me, he has a wicked hand. Once I've been punished, then I am forgiven. But, every night, I fall asleep in their arms, nestled between them, loved and happy. It might be different for you. I've never had anyone who cares for me, at least, not that I can remember. Now to have two men of my own? It's as though a dream I never knew I had has come true. Will you be all right?"

"I honestly don't know but, at least, I won't have to worry about him coming home drunk and having to lock him out of the spring house. He wanted to do vile things to me, like what he wanted you to do." She shuddered.

"What he wanted to do wasn't vile, he was. Find some happiness, Sally. You deserve it," Elizabeth said.

Caelan joined them, wrapping his arm around Lizzie. "Aye, Sally. Be happy, if ye can, and thank you again. Ye didna have to worry about yer husband. We'll take care of it."

7

THEY WATCHED her as she walked to the path down the side of the hill and waved as the sheriff's widow rode away.

"Jesus, Gavan. If his wife had not shot him..."

"Lizzie would have been fine. We weren't far behind, and our bride had the good sense to play him along. I'm not sure how she's going to feel about sucking cock for a while, but she's strong, and she does enjoy it."

"Ye think we should let her be tonight?"

Gavan shook his head. "No, I fear if we let her get it in her head that she did something wrong, or that we don't want her because of it, it could be months, or years, before she gets over it."

Caelan bristled. "But if that's what it takes for her to heal?" he growled.

"Calm yerself, Cae. We'll give our girl whatever she needs for as long as she needs it. But she's going to need us to be strong for her, as well. Ye do know she had no choice, right?"

"Do ye want me to punch ye in the nose again?" he snarled.

"Why would you punch Gav in the nose? Again?" she asked, joining them.

Gavan hung his head. "He had every right to punch me. When I found ye gone, I thought ye had run away…"

She surprised them both by laughing. "I'll bet you were furious," she said, trying not to giggle, but failing. She turned to Caelan, "Did he threaten to beat me within an inch of my life?"

Caelan started to chuckle while Gavan glowered. "Nay, I think what he said he was planning to welt yer pretty arse and then fuck ye until ye couldn't walk."

Lizzie approached Gavan and wrapped her arms around him. "That sounds nice, except for the welting my ass part. But the fucking me until I can't walk sounds lovely. Would ye carry me around, then, husband?" she said mocking his brogue.

"Yer Scottish brogue is getting very good, wife. Would ye really like to be fucked so hard ye canna walk the next day?"

Caelan's heart clutched when he saw the fear flash across her face. She was still clinging to Gavan, who had his arms around her. Caelan joined them wrapping his arms around her from the back. "It's okay Lizzie, we can let ye have some time."

Gavan nodded.

She shook her head. "I don't want time. I want both of you. I want to know that seeing me on my knees sucking Gutherie's..."

"Shh, Lizzie. We both told ye how proud of ye we are. Had ye not had the courage and tenacity to do what ye did, we'd have lost ye," crooned Gavan.

"He's right, lass. I didna know many women who would have had your strength and cunning to buy us the time we needed to find you," said Caelan, softly nuzzling her neck and bringing his hands up to cup her breasts, kneading them.

She wriggled her derriere into his groin as his cock started to swell. He and Gavan weren't just telling her what she wanted to hear. She'd shown such bravery in dealing with Gutherie. He was so very proud to call her his wife. He could feel Gavan squeezing her buttocks.

"Aye, lass, I have rarely known anyone, man or woman, who could have done what ye did. Ye deserve better than me to have doubted ye. Can ye find it in your heart to forgive me?" Gavan whispered.

Caelan knew that confession had cost him and prayed that Lizzie did as well.

Lizzie landed a hard smack on Gavan's buttocks. "What is it ye always tell me? Once I've paid the consequences for my behavior and have been forgiven, that's the end of it. Well, I've forgiven ye, and I expect that to be the end of it."

Gavan chuckled, lust underlying his tone. "Have ye, now? I think, Cae, our bride's getting a bit too big for her britches again."

"Best we get her back to our camp and get her out of them," Caelan agreed.

"Ye take her. I'll deal with the sheriff…"

"No," said Lizzie. "I don't want to be apart from either of you."

Gavan kissed the tip of her nose. "Nay. It's not something I want you to see or be involved with. Ye go with Cae and be a good girl. If we're to leave tomorrow, there's work to be done at the camp, and ye can help him with it."

"But you won't be long?" she asked.

"Nay, lass, I'll be back and, then, Cae and I will show ye how very much ye are loved by yer husbands."

"Come, Lizzie. Let Gavan do what needs doing. He'll be along right quick now that he knows yer wanting some lovin' from both of us."

He led her to his horse and helped her mount, swinging up behind her and nodding to Gavan.

––––––––

GAVAN

Gavan waited until they were well away before taking his pistol and putting a bullet through the same hole as Sally. He tied the sheriff's body over his horse and then found a likely spot to stage the sheriff's death. When he was satisfied with the outcome, he turned the horse loose and shooed him on his way. The horse would run home, thus initiating the search for the sheriff.

After he'd completed his chore, making sure no trace of what had really transpired remained, he returned to their camp to find Lizzie helping Caelan clean freshly caught fish. He was unsaddling his horse and putting him in the corral when Caelan joined him.

"We need to talk about Lizzie."

"She seemed fine up at the cavern, did something happen once ye got back?" asked Gavan, concerned.

"Not like acting out, but I get a sense that mask of bravado we saw at her trial has come back. I think she's feeling bad guilty about Gutherie."

"She did what she had to do..."

"I agree. She made a comment about if she'd been where we told her. And, regardless of what she's says, I think she feels it was wrong to put her mouth on another man."

"She has a point, at least about having ventured past where we told her. Do ye think she feels like she needs to be spanked?"

"Aye, I do."

"Then, it's up to us to give her what she needs."

They finished getting the horses bedded down for the night.

"Lizzie?" Gavan called and she looked up. "Come here, wife," he said in a mildly stern tone.

She joined them. "Did you see the riding skirt Cae got me, and the pretty blouse? He bought me a new chemise, corset, stockings, and boots as well."

"Aye, Caelan tends to spoil ye, even when ye've been naughty."

"Naughty?"

Gavan nodded. "Were ye not told to not go beyond the bend in the river?"

"Yes, but..."

" 'Tis yer butt that's going to pay the price. Gavan and I talked it over and we think, if ye'd minded us, the sheriff might not have snatched ye. While we're proud of how ye handled yerself, I think ye'd agree that yer still owed a spanking for your disobedience. Don't ye?"

Gavan's heart broke when she nodded, tears welling in her eyes.

"I wouldn't have had to..." She stopped herself.

"Ye wouldn't have had to what? Do whatever ye had to in order to survive? Stall for time so we could find ye? Did ye lie to us about yer feelings about this afternoon?"

"Maybe a little," she admitted.

"Maybe, then, we were wrong not to spank yer pretty bottom," said Caelan. "Take yer clothes off, Lizzie, and come put yer hands on the log."

"I thought you said a spanking..."

"I did. Get yerself naked and come get in position. We're going to spank yer bottom in tandem."

Gavan realized Caelan was right. Lizzie needed to be spanked to atone for whatever she felt she'd done wrong. Even though they disagreed with her, she needed this, and they would provide what she needed.

Once she was in place, they took up a position on either side of her.

"I think her arse is the wrong color, Cae, don't ye?"

"Aye, it's far too fair. And she's an arse just made for her husbands. There'll come a time, Lizzie, that ye'll get yer arse fucked when ye've misbehaved on top of yer spanking but, since yer not ready for that, we'll just have to put enough sting in yer tail to make it count."

————

LIZZIE

SHE PLACED her hands on the log, making her body perpendicular to it. She took a deep breath and exhaled it in a yowl, propelling her up on her tiptoes when both of their hands landed harsh strikes to her ass at the same.

Caelan took off his bandana and stuffed it into her mouth. "Ye'll take yer punishment with a bit more grace and a lot less noise than ye usually do."

They began landing one blow after another on her backside. First Gavan and then Caelan; first one side and then the other.

She bit the kerchief to keep from screaming. Nothing had ever hurt so bad or felt so good and so right. Left! Right! Smack! Thwack! They walloped her behind until she couldn't tell if she was in heaven, or hell.

The pain was intense, but so was the arousal knowing they loved and cared for her enough to give her what she needed. With each swat that landed, her pussy throbbed in anticipation and need. Desire for these two men coursed through her veins and, each time one of their hands landed, it not only added to the fire they were ignighting all across her ass, but deepened her commitment to them and increased her need for their passion and dominance.

She hadn't realized they had stopped until she felt Gavan's two fingers penetrate her.

"Ach, Cae," he chuckled. "Our wife's cunny is drenched."

Gavan brought his finger up, teased her back entrance for a moment before sinking in up to his second knuckle.

Lizzie lost her grip on the kerchief and screamed as her body convulsed in a powerful orgasm, almost driving her to her knees.

Cae leaned down and whispered, "I can't wait to get ye home and in our bed, Lizzie, and sink my cock deep into yer arse. And, after ye've had both of us that way a couple of times, Gav's going to fill yer cunny while I fill yer arse. Feel this?" he said, withdrawing his finger and spanking her ass again, followed quickly by Gavan striking the other.

They returned to their rhythmic spanking as she began to howl and her tears fell freely.

"Ye were a naughty wife. Now, instead of being over in our bed having supper and fucking, we have to deal with yer disobedience. Do ye think that's fair, Lizzie?" Gavan growled.

"No, Gavan, I'm sorry. I should have stayed where you told me."

"Aye, lass, ye should have," agreed Caelan.

They continued to spank and scold her for venturing past the point they'd told her to stay until she was sobbing and wailing, promising to never do it again.

"Ye think she's learned her lesson?" Gavan asked Caelan.

"Not quite. Give her cunny a good finger fucking

while I get the bigger plug. I've got supper almost ready. We'll put the plug in, and she can wear it the rest of the night."

Gavan nodded. "And she wanted to be fucked until she couldn't walk. I'll sit her on my lap with my cock up her cunny and she can eat that way. When we're done, you can have her first."

"That's generous of you."

" 'Tis only fair. I'll have her soft sheath embracing my cock through supper, and I suspect she'll come a time or two, especially if we suck her nipples."

"That usually does it for her."

"So you fuck her first."

It was Gavan's turn to lean down to their bride. "When he's done with ye, I'll make sure ye canna walk tomorrow."

Lizzie had no time for any kind of words to form. She had already been practically incoherent and telling her what they planned only inflamed her lust.

When Caelan left them, Gavan immediately began to finger fuck her with two fingers, ensuring his fingers were spread wide as he did so. As he thrust them into her, her inner walls quivered and shook as she tried to make sense of what had happened. She had disobeyed her husbands and almost gotten killed for her trouble. She was being punished in the most wickedly sensual way.

Her breath sped up, and the noises she was making became little whimpers as her orgasm approached faster than she could fathom. Her muscles tensed, and her toes curled in anticipation. Her breathing became labored and she began to pant, terrified of the amount of pleasure her husbands were set on inflicting.

Suddenly, she fell over the edge as he gave one hard, ferocious thrust deep inside her. Screaming in ecstasy, her pussy spasmed. Clamping down hard, her legs trembling as she fought to remain standing, bent over at the junction of her body and thighs. The orgasm went on and on, until she was begging for it to end, not sure if she could take any more. The little tremors racing through her body afterwards made her whimper.

Caelan held the plug in front of her. "Suck and lick it, Lizzie, as though it were my cock. If I were ye, I'd make sure it was plenty wet as that is all the lubricant ye'll get before I shove it in your bottom hole and fuck ye with it before I finish in yer pussy."

"You'll pull it out before Gavan…"

"That's up to Gavan."

Gavan's malevolent chuckle told her there'd be no respite there.

Caelan held up the plug, and Lizzie began to suck and lick it, making sure it was plenty wet. Once it was sufficiently slick, Caelan slowly inserted it into her bottom hole.

She took deep breaths, forcing her body to relax and take the plug. "Caelan," she moaned.

He chuckled. "Ye know, Gav, I canna tell if she wants me to stop, or see if I canna get it deeper."

"Caelan, please, I need…"

"What do ye need, Lizzie? Do ye need me to fill yer pussy with my cock? Do ye want me and Gavan to ride ye hard until ye decide yer going to mind yer husbands?"

"Yes, please?" she mewled.

Lizzie was in desperate need to be fucked, and fucked hard. Caelan knew he and Gavan could more than satisfy that need.

Caelan stepped squarely behind her and swatted her pussy with his hard hand. She yowled but remained in place.

Out of the corner of his eye, he could see Gavan watching them intently, his cock straining against the front of his trousers. There was no doubt in Caelan's mind that Lizzie was going to get the fucking she needed.

"Nay, lass," he growled. "Ye were warned not to go beyond the bend of the river. Ye disobeyed Gavan and almost got yerself killed. I mean to mount you like a stallion mounts his mare and fuck your pussy raw before Gav does the same. Yer lucky we aren't at home, else Gav would be in yer pussy, and I'd be having yer arse."

With no other preliminaries, Caelan stepped forward, guided his cock to the entrance of her core and thrust forward ferociously, forcing her sheath to accommodate all of him and extracting a powerful climax just from his possession. He grunted with satisfaction as he gripped her hip with one hand and slid the hand that had been on her neck to the top of her shoulder to hold her in place as he began to take long, deep strokes.

Lizzie felt as though she had been split her in two. Each time as he drove forward, she could swear the head of his staff rammed into the end of her sheath. There was no relief for her, as he had her trapped. All she could do was submit to his rough claiming, to soften her body so as to make it more receptive to his and to agree without words to his dominant possession. She knew, if Caelan was this intent on fucking her as part of his punishment, Gavan would be far worse, and she needed him to be.

Caelan's cock stroked her over and over as he grunted and groaned in satisfaction. "Jesus, Lizzie. Yer cunt squeezing my cock feels so good."

Without warning, her entire body convulsed, and her pussy contracted all along his length pulsing in the same rhythm that he plunged in and out of her. She could feel him pushing her to the edge. He was forcing her to accept pleasure from him in the same way as he forced her obedience. She winced each time his hips slammed into her heated backside as his cock scraped her cunny walls.

Even her repeated climaxes, and the copious amount of her honey that he demanded she give him, were not enough to completely negate the ravaging his cock was giving her pussy. Roughly, he began fucking her with more fury and speed. She felt her body gearing up to meet his in triumphant climax.

Plunging in and out of her he roared.

She screamed his name as she tumbled over the abyss into an ecstasy she had never known before. She felt her mind and spirit leave her body and watched as if from above as he thrust into her three more times before his cock erupted, emptying his essence deep inside her.

When he was finished, he withdrew from her, his cock was covered with their comingled creamy response to his possession and dripping the last remnants of his seed.

"Yer a good lass. Ye give Gavan the best fuck he ever had." He grinned at his friend as he jiggled the butt plug, making her wail. "She's primed for ye, Gav. Fuck her hard and see that she takes to heart the lesson of what happens to disobedient wives."

"Get out of the way, Cae," Gavan growled.

———

GAVAN

He pulled Lizzie to her feet and tossed her over his shoulder, transporting her back to their bed. He meant to give her a good ramming. He knelt, laying her down none too gently and palming her breasts, tweaking and pinching her nipples. He climbed over and lowered himself between her thighs, mounting her with one, hard plunge to her depths.

Lizzie screamed again just as she had when Caelan had mounted her. She reached up and clutched at him as she came hard from nothing other than his ramming his cock home. Her legs wrapped around his, and he settled into a strong rhythm of thrusting.

He stroked her, feeling her pussy quiver and tried to remember if there had ever been a time he'd enjoyed fucking a woman even half this much. He reached under her and took hold of her sore bottom to hold her steady so he could extract the maximum amount of pleasure she could give him.

He heard her breathing speed up and lose its rhythm.

She began to pant shallowly in unison with his grunting as he plowed her.

He focused on the way she responded to keep from spilling himself too soon. Gavan felt her body stiffen in anticipation of her rapidly approaching orgasm.

She threw back her head and cried out in ecstasy as he thrust ferociously into her hot, wet heat.

Giving one final thrust, her pussy spasmed and trembled all along his cock as he pumped his seed deep inside her. His climax seemed to last forever.

She clung to him and whimpered as her cunt continued to have little mini-climaxes and encouraged him to deposit every last drop of his cum and stay coupled with her.

He uncoupled from her, sat up with his back against the headboard, and then dragged her over his lap, forcing her down on his semi-erect cock.

Lizzie collapsed against him and lay her head on his shoulder.

He wrapped his arms around her waist, allowing his hands to rest lightly on her ass.

"Ye didna mind me today, and it almost cost ye yer life. Come tomorrow morning, ye'll be sore and tired, but we're leaving for home, anyway. I don't want to hear one word of complaint from ye. If ye ever blatantly disobey me again where it's a question of safety, I'll welt yer ass before Caelan fucks it. Understood?"

Lizzie nodded, nuzzled his neck, and settled herself in his lap, on his cock, and in their lives.

Caelan joined them and handed Gavan a bottle of whiskey he had with them. He kissed her head.

"Ye scared the shit out of us. Ye could have been killed. Never do it again," he scolded.

She reached for Caelan's hand with hers. "I won't. I'm so, so sorry."

Both men kissed simultaneously. "Forgiven," they said in unison.

"Let that be the end of it, Lizzie. Ye ken?" admonished Gavan in a soft, but stern voice.

"Aye," she said, cuddling up even closer as she fell asleep.

Gavan never moved that night. Lizzie slept and, for the first time, didn't have bad dreams to disturb her rest.

———

LIZZIE

THE NEXT MORNING, she woke in their bedroll alone. Alarmed, she sat up and called for them.

Caelan stood up by the campfire, "Lizzie, ye all right?"

She stood, ran to him and wrapped her arms around his body. "I woke up, and neither of you was there."

"Of course not, ye lazy bones, 'tis well into the morning, and we're leaving for home today." Caelan saw the concern in her eyes and kissed her gently. "What's troubling ye?"

Lizzie snuggled against him. "Nothing," and then yelped when his hand connected with her backside.

"What have ye been told about lying?"

"Truly nothing. I'm just not used to at least one of you being there snuggling with me."

"Ye didn't have a lot of snuggling or affection when ye were growing up, did ye, lass?"

She shook her head. "No. You and Gav are the only ones I ever remember caring about me, wanting to make sure I was happy."

He squeezed her tight. "Then, we'll just have to make up for lost time."

She smiled up at him. "Where's Gav?"

"He had a quick errand to run. I suspect he'll be back any time now. There he is," he said pointing to the opening in the canyon.

Caelan was right. Gavan was astride his big appaloosa horse leading a beautiful palomino behind him. Not just any palomino, but her palomino. The one that had been taken from her when she was captured and jailed.

"Outlaw!" she cried, clapping her hands together and laughing.

She turned to Caelan and threw her arms around him, hugging him close, before spinning away and running toward Gavan.

Gavan stopped and reached down to grab her, hoisting her over the saddle in front of him and delivering a sharp blow to her backside.

"Ye didna run up to horses naked and with bare feet," he scolded as he rode over to Caelan and handed her down. "Ye go get dressed."

"No," she said.

"Lizzie..." Caelan warned. "He didna get fucked this morning, he may not be in the mood for any of yer sass."

"He's not the only one..." she said, her eyes gleaming with mirth and lust.

"Ach, so now yer telling yer husbands yer feeling neglected."

She giggled. "How could any woman who has the two most wonderful husbands in the world feel that? But I did miss both of you this morning."

"Well, had my errand not taken longer than I expected, I might be willing to indulge your wanton nature, but we've a long ride ahead of us if we mean to get to Bridgewater tomorrow."

Caelan wrapped her in his arms, one going up to roll her distended nipple between his fingers, and the other stealing down to slip between her legs.

"Ye want us to get home, don't ye, Lizzie? Ye want both of yer husbands' cocks deep inside; Gav in yer pussy, and me in yer arse?"

Lizzie leaned back into his strength and warmth, closing her eyes and reveling in his embrace. "Aye. I'm afraid ye married yerselves a wanton hussy who can't seem to get enough of her husbands."

The two men chuckled.

She opened her eyes and looked at Gavan. "But where did you find Outlaw? They sold him when I was captured."

"I tracked down the new owner and bought him back. They had your saddle, and other gear, as well, so I bought that, too. Turns out, Cae, our Lizzie isn't the only one with a naughty streak. This beast of hers has not allowed anyone to ride him."

"He's kind of funny about that," she admitted, grinning. She crooked her finger at Gavan, "Will you please come see me, so I don't get spanked for getting too close without boots on?"

Gavan grinned. "Ye'd look fine in just a pair of boots, lass," he said, his brogue thickening as it always did when he was becoming aroused.

She hugged him and kissed him, "Thank you."

"Well, ye needed a horse to ride..."

"Not for the horse, well, for him, too, but for everything; for keeping me safe and for loving me when I didn't know how to love anyone, even myself."

Caelan came up from behind and hugged her so that she stood in the strong and loving embrace of her two husbands.

8

IZZIE

Six months had passed since they returned home with their bride. They had been welcomed home by the others at Bridgewater with much fanfare.

At first, Lizzie had been unsure of herself with the other women and was most comfortable when she was with either Gavan or Caelan. Little by little that had faded as she realized these women were far more like her than one would think at first.

Gavan and Caelan had spent a long day, moving the herd from one part of the ranch to another. There had been a general meeting of everyone at the ranch before the women split off to let the men discuss business.

"Come on, Lizzie. Let the men have their cigars and whiskey. We'll have a nice cup of tea and talk about them," said Emma, Ian and Kane's wife. "You can work with me on perfecting my brogue. I have to say, it has the most delightful effect on Ian when whispered into his ear when he's fucking me."

Lizzie giggled and spent an entertaining evening with the other wives, regaling them with tales of her outlaw days.

When Gavan had come to collect her, she had been genuinely sorry to be the first to go.

When they went to mount up, Lizzie said, "Where's Cae?"

"He went on ahead to prepare a bath for all three of us. We've been working hard all day and thought we could use a bath."

"What about me?" she'd teased.

"Yer our favorite bath toy."

Caelan was just finishing filling the large bathtub when they arrived. Lizzie had never thought she'd live in such a beautiful, comfortable and luxurious home. She took great pride in keeping it clean and taking care of her two husbands.

Lizzie went into their bedroom and undressed down to her corset and chemise. Caelan and Gavan had decided she would not wear bloomers. They were far too fond of being able to get their hands on her short curls, which they had decided to keep, and fingering her cunny, often bringing the honey they found there to their mouths to taste.

She was allowed to get undressed without their assistance, but only down to her undergarments. They had fallen into a pattern where Caelan would hold her with her front to his back, much as Gavan had that first night. Then, Gavan would slowly unlace her corset as he kissed the tops of her shoulders and her neck and removed it. Lizzie's freed breasts would be tantalizingly fondled by Caelan as Gavan maneuvered her out of her chemise.

"Were ye a good lass today while we were gone?" Caelan asked.

That, too, had become ritual. Her husbands had found that there were times she needed to be spanked, even if she hadn't disobeyed them. There was something fundamental, and profound, about having her bottom blistered that reassured her and kept her from acting out.

"No, I was a good girl, today," she replied leaning back against his hard chest.

He turned her around to face him. Gavan caressed her ass, and she felt his hard cock run along her spine as Caelan pressed her down and offered his cock to her mouth.

"Open," he said.

Lizzie licked her lips and did as she'd been bid.

Caelan pushed his cock past her lips and teeth to the back of her throat, groaning as he did.

Gavan steadied her head in order to keep her still so that Caelan could languidly fuck her mouth.

They might keep her head from moving, but Lizzie used her tongue and her ability to suck to pleasure him. She was rewarded when he groaned heavily, and his staff began to twitch and pulse in her mouth.

Gavan moved his hands down to her shoulders as

Caelan grasped her hair in his hands, using her mouth more forcefully as she tasted the first drop of his pre-cum.

At first, she had resisted swallowing their cum, but they had insisted and, when she protested, she'd been soundly spanked. Now, she accepted they would send their cum into whatever receptacle they chose; mouth, pussy, or ass. She didn't particularly like the taste, but it pleased them, and she was given no choice in the matter.

Caelan rocked his hips, driving into her mouth.

Lizzie focused on relaxing her jaw so she could take him more deeply as he increased his tempo.

Calen made noises of deep male gratification and arousal as he took her mouth; it was music to her ears. His cock seemed to swell as it began shooting his load down her throat. He tasted salty, yet sweet, and his cum going down her gullet and into her belly was warm and satisfying.

When he finished, he opened his eyes and looked down at her and over at Gavan. They often reversed who fucked her mouth, with the other getting his choice of which of her other two pleasure portals he wanted to fuck.

Slowly, Caelan withdrew from her mouth, and Gavan leaned down to pick her up and take her into the bath where he set her in the water.

"Scoot forward," he said.

As she did so, Gavan stepped into the tub behind her and lowered himself into the water, with Caelan doing the same, except in front of and facing her.

Leaning against his chest, Gavan would wrap her in his arms as she laid her head on his shoulder. She could feel his hard cock pressing against her as he picked up the washcloth and began to bathe both of them.

Caelan did the same, never taking his eyes off of them and often reaching over to caress her. Gavan, for the most part, seemed content to just hold her and allow her to luxuriate in the water.

She closed her eyes and relaxed against him.

The water began to cool, and she took both of his hands, which were holding the sides of the tub, and brought them down to her breasts.

Gavan enclosed both of her mounds, squeezing gently before tracing circles around her areolas and then rolling her already stiff nipples between his strong fingers.

Lizzie moaned again, but this time in arousal, and not in relaxation.

Gavan continued to massage her left tit as he trailed his right index finger down the centerline of her body and through the patch of hair covering her mons. He deftly probed until he found her clit and began to mimic with it what he was doing to her left nipple.

Lizzie squirmed and was rewarded by him pinching both stiffened nubs until she quelled her own need and lay back against him. "Gavan?"

"Aye, Lizzie?" he murmured.

"Are you going to keep me in this chilly water, just playing around, or are we going to get out, get in bed, and fuck?" She leaned over to Caelan, taking his semi-erect member in her hand and squeezing gently. "I may not have needed to be spanked, but I do need to be fucked."

He smiled. "Who decides when ye get fucked?"

She pouted, "You, or Gavan."

He nodded. "And who does the fucking?"

"You and Gavan," she said, hearing Gavan's sexy chuckle behind her and anticipating the next question.

"And who gets fucked?"

"I do."

"There's a good lass," said Gavan as he stood and exited the tub, offering her his hand. "Do ye think our bride has been good enough to have her way with us?"

Caelan laughed. "Never, but I'm damn well horny enough that I mean to give her a good ramming. What do ye say you take her cunny, and I'll have her arse?"

Lizzie inhaled sharply. There was something deeply satisfying about having the two of them fucking her at the same time.

They stood her in front of the fire, each holding her wrapped in a towel until they were dried off and had her dried as well.

"Ye do realize, Lizzie, that yer the only woman the laird there has ever loved."

Gavan snorted. "As opposed to the plowboy who loved anything that offered her cunny, or arse, to fuck."

She smiled, but wisely decided to remain silent. Even though she stood beside them in front of the fire being dried by them both, she was not a part of the conversation. This was between them and, while they loved her, they loved each other as well. Their love didn't include fucking, or touching, each other, but it was as profound as the love they each bore for her. She was the most important thing in this life to each and both of them. They all cared for the others and, by sharing her, they had created a family, and a life. Lizzie, who had spent so much of her life alone, was now the center of their world and basked in their light.

Gavan led her to the bed. "On your knees, Lizzie. I mean to suck yer cunny while Cae gets yer arse ready. Yer going to get fucked by both yer husbands tonight."

"Will I be sore in the morning?"

"Aye, good and sore. I've been wanting you all day, as has Caelan."

"I like the sound of that. Two husbands, two cocks," Lizzie purred.

She was fairly sure there was nothing better in this world than having one husband licking her pussy, supping up her honey, while the other ensured her ass was prepared to take his large cock and then being impaled on both at the same time.

Gavan rolled her to her side, and she got up on her knees so that her bottom was elevated. He lifted one of her legs and slid underneath her, his own legs hanging off the edge.

The feel of his hot breath just below her cunny made her moan with arousal.

He pulled her down onto his face, his tongue plunging directly into her wet heat.

She continued to moan as he began to lick her cunny.

He delved inside, sucking at the lips outside her core, nibbling on one, and then kissing and nuzzling the other. Pleasure blossomed throughout her entire body, firing the synapses of her nerves and making her feel as though she outshone the brightest stars.

She'd survived whole. Lizzie was deeply grateful that

her husbands understood what she had done with Gutherie and how it affected her. She had needed their spanking and rough fucking that afternoon, and they had given her what she needed, even though everything in them had wanted only to love and comfort her.

Gavan continued to lick her sex with pleasure.

Caelan rubbed the globes of her ass before parting her cheeks. He dipped his fingers in some salve that he used to ease his way into her ass if Gavan was going to be taking her cunny at the same time.

"Let me get ye nice and slick, sweetheart." Caelan's voice caressing her in the same way as his hands, or Gavan's mouth. It raced along her skin, raising goosebumps as he kissed the small of her back. "Breathe, lass, and stay soft for me. I can't wait to be inside you."

Lizzie felt her pussy pulsing as Gavan licked the swollen nub at the apex of her thighs, drawing his tongue across the bundled nerves and bringing her to climax as Caelan worked the salve in. Lizzie was caught in a vortex of emotional and physical feeling between the soft work of Gavan's tongue and the erotic caress of Caelan's fingers as he rimmed her dark rosette. Her toes curled, and she felt her impending climax. So much sensation and sensory overload. She closed her eyes, trying to ride the wave.

"She's so tight. She's going to feel so good," murmured Caelan to no one in particular as he sank his finger up to the knuckle and plunged it in and out in a gentle motion. "Don't fight me, lass. Ye know ye want me inside ye as much as I do."

Lizzie tried to relax. He was right. Although it was

hard to admit and often was uncomfortable, especially at first, she had come to crave Caelan's cock up her arse in the same way she wanted Gavan's in her cunny. Best of all was when she had them both at the same time.

Gavan continued to fuck her with his tongue, stabbing up inside her core before moving to her nub and suckling.

Lizzie was too close to the edge and, as Caelan continued to finger her dark passage, she slipped over the edge, Gavan's mouth shooting sparks of pure carnal ecstasy through her system. Her body shuddered as she cried out as her orgasm enveloped her.

Before she could recover, they were moving her into position, adjusting theirs before she'd even had a chance to completely ride the crest of her climax.

Gavan rolled out from under her and propped himself on the pillows in front of the iron headboard they had crafted for their enormous bed.

His cock was proud and strong, silently calling to her to impale herself.

"Come here, lass. Let's get my cock settled in yer cunny."

Caelan gave her a hand, helping her move over Gavan's body.

Lizzie straddled his body with her thighs and, bracing her hands on his chest, lowered herself onto his rigid staff.

"Aye, Lizzie, that's it. When yer cunny and arse are still dripping our seed, I'll fuck your mouth and tickle that soft spot at the back of your throat. Ye'll get everything I have, and more; but, for now, ye'll give me what I want."

He grasped her hips and pulled down, impaling her on his cock. He was so swollen, she had to work her way down, forcing him in, inch by tantalizing inch. He filled her until she might have questioned if Caelan would have room, but she knew he wouldn't be denied. "This is where I want to be all the time, Lizzie."

Gavan's hips surged upward, making her see shooting stars in her mind's eye as her body achieved a kind of perfect storm of feeling and emotion. She'd already come, but she was racing again toward the abyss of pleasure they always provided.

Caelan placed his hand on her spine and pushed her forward gently.

"Lean forward, lass. Smash your nipples against Gav's chest. Him and that monster cock he's got shoved up yer cunny aren't giving me a lot of room."

"So you can get your monster cock shoved up my ass?" she teased.

"Exactly," he agreed.

Caelan's hand pressed against her back. Her nipples rubbed against Gavan's chest, the dark hair stimulating them.

Gavan kissed her, his tongue dancing with hers as Caelan pressed his cock to the tight ring of muscle that guarded her ass.

She whimpered a little as he started to push inside.

His cock, working its way in, was part pain, part pleasure, and all dominance in its most carnal, erotic form. Lizzie willed herself to relax and allowed him to take what he wanted because she wanted to give it to him.

Lizzie flattened her back, wanting to feel both of her husbands inside her body, taking pleasure from their possession.

"Fuck, she's tight," said Caelan as the head of his cock slipped inside her dark passage.

He held himself there, allowing her body to adjust and accept his penetration and knowing, in those few moments, he was driving her wild with desire. Lizzie felt so open and free, possessed and bound to them both.

"Cae, please," she mewled, believing she would die if they both didn't start working the respective hole they'd claimed.

Lizzie moaned and writhed in their dual embrace. She always reveled in their lovemaking, but this was different. It was unlike anything she'd ever felt before.

"Hush, now. Let me take my time with ye. Ye feel so good. So tight. So absolutely fucking right. Do ye have any idea how happy ye make us?"

Caelan pressed in, filling her with his cock.

Lizzie fought every instinct and need she had to begin to move on their cocks on her own but knew that would result in both of them withdrawing, her getting spanked and punished. Wanting to avoid that, she forced herself to obey and remained still.

She hated and loved this strange mix of pleasure, pain, fullness, and intimacy. She felt trapped in the most hedonistic and purest way possible.

Caelan continued to press forward until she could

feel his balls resting against her. Both of her husbands were as deep as possible,

Suddenly curious, she asked, "Can you feel him?"

Gavan grinned, softening the angular lines of his face. "Yeah. Yer so tight this way. I can feel him when he's moving and sliding his cock into ye. Mere words cannot express what I share with the two of ye. Well, maybe one: perfection."

"Are you ready, lass?" Caelan asked.

She'd been ready for this forever. "Yes, a thousand times yes."

Caelan pulled out, and Lizzie felt her fingers sink into Gavan's biceps. The feel of his withdrawal was so incredible. It was difficult to let him in, but the slow pull of his cock as he neared the end of her dark channel caused her nerve endings to flare, firing shock waves of pleasure throughout her body.

As Caelan pulled out, Gavan flexed his hips up, grinding his groin against her clit.

Then, they began to rock her in the most profound embrace, perfectly in tune with one another. They achieved a pounding rhythm of melody and harmony created by their bodies and in perfect tempo with her own.

Lizzie closed her eyes and relinquished control completely.

They pushed and pulled, bringing her to the edge of ecstasy again and again and not ever letting her soar free in time and space. They kept her soul tethered to them in the same way her body was anchored by theirs. Their cocks thrusted in and out, pounding in time, until she wasn't sure who was causing which sensation. The only thing she knew was she wanted more. Every way she moved created a new feeling, her arse and her cunny skating the rim of a deep canyon of carnal bliss.

Gavan pressed up again, demanding she capitulate and let her orgasm take her.

Lizzie wailed, pushing back and taking Caelan in and then moving forward to extract the maximum pleasure Gavan's cock could provide.

Calen grunted behind her, his hot seed filling her arse.

A second later, Gavan followed, his cock pumping his seed into her until he had nothing left.

Lizzie fell forward, completely exhausted, utterly spent, and wholly happy.

"Good, girl," Caelan crooned, settling in behind her.

Gavan held her close. "Are ye all right? We weren't too rough?"

She shook her head, unable to speak. She was finally at peace in a way she never could have expected. The girl who had once vowed to never depend on anyone but herself was now completely and totally dependent on the two men who had saved her from the hangman. But they made sure, each and every way, to let her know that they, too, felt as though she had saved them, and the three of them would face whatever life threw at them together as one.

**BRIDGEWATER
BRIDES**

Want more Bridgewater Brides?
See the full list of books in the world:
http://bridgewaterbrides.com/books/

Be sure to sign up for the world newsletter to stay up to
date on new releases:
http://bridgewaterbrides.com/mailing-list/

ABOUT DELTA JAMES

Sinfully sultry romance - that's the world that International and US best-selling author Delta James inhabits and shares with her readers. A world where alpha heroes find true love with feisty heroines. Delta's stories are filled with erotic encounters of romance and discipline. One fan suggested it was best to have a "fan and a glass of water" when reading Delta's stories.

Delta has been a highly successful competitor both in horse shows (Arabians, Appaloosas and Paints) and in the AKC and International Kennel Club with her beloved basset hounds.

Delta is always happy to hear from those who enjoy her work - and even those who don't. She can be reached at deltajames-author@hotmail.com

To find other books by Vanessa Vale:
https://vanessavaleauthor.com/
To find other books by Delta James:
https://www.deltajames.com/

Social Media Links
Sign up for my newsletter:

https://dl.bookfunnel.com/cpuo10j8s1
Like my Facebook page:
https://www.facebook.com/DeltaJamesAuthor/
Follow me on Bookbub:
https://www.bookbub.com/authors/delta-james
Follow me on Goodreads:
https://www.goodreads.com/author/show/
18197022.Delta_James
Twitter:
https://twitter.com/DeltaJamesBooks

9 781393 492955